Claimed

Evermore Series, Volume 2

Andrea Smith

Published by Andrea Smith, 2021.

<u>About the Author</u>

ANDREA SMITH

Claimed

Book #2 - Evermore Series

By Andrea Smith

Introduction

I have fallen in love with YA/NA Romance and Suspense. I got the idea for "Crushed" from something that happened many years ago, to someone I knew very well. I hope you enjoy the story.

This is Book 2 in the "Evermore Series." It is a serial meaning that each novella needs to be read in order for the complete story.

1) Crushed
2) Claimed
3) Paparazzi
4) Star F*cking

Legal Stuff

Acknowledgments

Edited by: Ashley Blaschak Stout
Formatted by: Erik Gevers
Cover Design: Freya Barker

Table of Contents

Dedication

This book is dedicated to my friend, Terri Ball, who gave me the encouragement and support during some of the roughest times. Thank you, Terri.

R.I.P.

Recap

Feel free to skip if everything from Book 1, is still fresh in your mind!

In Book 1, "Crushed," we are introduced to Neilah Grace Evans, aged 13 when the story begins. Known as Neely, she has been uprooted from Tennessee when her father lands a job at a prestigious law firm in L.A., one that focuses primarily on entertainment law.

An only child, Neely has pretty much always had her own interests with which to occupy her time. That doesn't change once the family relocates to Malibu, California two years prior.

Seth Drake is fourteen when "Crushed" begins, and has been Neely's best friend from down the beach since shortly after her arrival. They swim in her pool, go to the pier to fish, hang out on the beach, and take the same school bus together.

The friendship eventually evolves into a first love situation between Neely and Seth. They enjoy one another's company more and more, and though they have distinctly different dreams for their futures, they find common ground in their present.

Seth's mother is an actress on a popular daytime soap, and Seth hopes to get into acting himself after college. That is his dream.

Neely, of course, wants to pursue her passion for art, specifically, painting in various medias, perhaps even becoming a teacher.

But things come to a crashing halt when Neely's mother starts drinking heavily, and the truth is exposed all over the tabloids that her father has been having an affair with a starlet, Tiffany Blume.

Her mother quickly flees California with her daughter in tow, hoping her husband comes to his senses and gives up the glitz and debauchery that comes with Hollywood.

It doesn't happen, though.

Her parents' divorce, and Neely finds herself back in Tennessee, away from her father, and from Seth, trying to pick up the pieces of her mother's life for her.

Fast-forward three years. Neely is now seventeen and has only visited California once since the divorce. That was the summer she was fifteen, and she spent a few weeks with her father.

During that time, things between Seth and herself heated up, but not to the point Seth would have liked. After a conversation with Laura, Seth's mother, Neely decided to cut her visit short. She left a break-up note for Seth, and returned the promise ring he had given her.

Now at seventeen, Neely has reconciled with her father after her mother enters rehab, and she finds herself once again in their home in Malibu.

Only everything has changed. Her father is now married to Tiffany Blume, and it is all Neely can do to remain civil to the glitzy actress. She has no desire to strike a bond with the woman who destroyed her family.

She has no clue where Seth is, or what he's doing, since she hasn't spoken to him for two years. She is determined to finish her senior year of high school and then find a college to attend where she won't have to remain under her father's roof any longer.

That's her plan anyway.

If she can just get through the next eight months without snapping off Tiffany Blume's head, she'll be out of there. She'll be on her way to becoming an adult, and carving a life out for herself. One that is free of the complications of emotional ties and family drama.

Chapter 1

Christmas Eve, 1996

"Neely, what do you think of these?" Tiffany called out from across the aisle at Nordstrom. I'd been busying myself flipping through a rack of neckties in search of one last gift for Dad.

I looked up and over, snapping my bubblegum loudly. It was a coping mechanism. The gum I mean. Every time I had to engage in some one-on-one time with Tiffany in order to make my father happy, I needed a wad of gum.

She held up a pair of plaid golf pants for my opinion. "Won't these be perfect for the cruise?" she asked in her bubbly voice.

"Yeah, they're great," I lied. "He'll love them."

He'll look like a complete dork, but he'll love them.

The last part was the absolute truth. My father loved everything about Tiffany. Her face, her body, her hair, her words, the air she exhaled. Well, I was probably overly exaggerating on *that* one, but the rest was true enough. I turned back to the ties, ready to make a selection.

"Or are these better?"

I looked back over to where she was now holding up a pair of bright celery green golf pants that had a bright yellow belt included. "You know, with his yellow Polo shirt. What do you think?"

She was looking at me expectantly, as if my opinion really mattered to her. "Definitely those," I said, putting some conviction in my voice. "I can picture Daddy in those perfectly."

I snickered inwardly. He'd look like something plucked from our garden back in Tennessee. What was it about adults turning pure idiot in the name of love? What magic spell had Tiffany woven so intricately with the delicate heartstrings of my father? It was all totally beyond me.

"Oh, what the hell," she said, releasing a hard sigh of indecision, "I'll get them both I guess. It's not like we can't afford them."

I shrugged and selected a royal blue silk tie for him. Now this was definitely my father. Just then a gaggle of ladies approached. Their stares and excited whispers gave them away immediately.

Fans.

It invariably happened no matter where Tiffany went. I often used that as a reason to beg off from accompanying her. I wish I had today, but her relentless whining had finally won me over.

"Are you *Tiffany Blume*?" the redheaded lady with dark blue eye shadow asked as the group closed in on my stepmother.

"Why yes," she gushed, giving them an appreciative smile, "yes I am."

"I told you, Elaine!" the lady continued, grabbing for a piece of paper from her shopping bag. "Would you mind terribly giving me your autograph? We all just love your show, Lotus Pointe. Watch it every Thursday night. I even record it on my VCR so I can watch it over and over again."

"So do I," a blonde woman in the group added. "I think you're the best female villain ever."

Tiffany was positively gushing as she took the pen and scribbled her autograph on the pieces of paper being thrust in her face.

"Will Austin come out of his coma before the season ends?" the redhead asked, her forehead creased in concern as if the actor who played Austin on the night time soap was actually in a freakin' coma.

Tiffany giggled her evil 'Libby' giggle—the character she played on Lotus Pointe—and handed the signed paper back to the woman. "Well, you know I'm not supposed to tell, and to be honest, even the cast has been kept in the dark on that one, but let's just say that the producers are trying to negotiate a new contract with Julian...I mean Austin," she corrected so the women would be clear on whom she was talking about, "and rumor has it it's not going well," she finished with a smug wink.

The blonde lady clearly wasn't happy with this little nugget of news, I could tell. I stood there silently and rolled my eyes. There wasn't anything on television that had ever fascinated me the way this show seemed to enrapture these women.

Truth was, I'd only watched about ten minutes of Lotus Pointe one time at Tiffany's prodding. It wasn't as if I wanted to see my stepmother's face or hear her voice anymore than I already did. But she'd whined until I had finally capitulated.

I think she wanted me to see just how villainous of a character she played. In retrospect, maybe that was her way of getting it across to me that she had it in her to be a force to contend with should I ever have the urge to challenge her position within our blended little family.

"They can't write Austin Benedict out!" the blonde woman finally blurted once the implications sunk in, "He's Cassidy Ryan's first love! What will happen to her if he dies?"

Oh, for Christ's sake!

Tiffany smiled and patted the woman's shoulder comfortingly. "Now don't despair. Remember, anything's possible in Hollywood, dear."

The women finally moved on, chatting away at the possibilities of what might happen with these fictional characters if the actor didn't sign a new contract with the studio.

"Sorry about that," Tiffany said, smiling in faux apology, "Just part of the job. I made a promise to myself long ago that I would always treat my fans with kindness and respect. They are, after all, my bread and butter."

"I guess," I replied, totally disinterested in the whole conversation, not to mention bored. "Are we ready to check out?"

"Oh, yes. Then how about we grab some lunch?"

Perfect.

Not.

"Sure," I conceded as I popped another piece of Bazooka into my mouth, "why not?"

Chapter 2

Tiffany insisted on driving to the Santa Monica Pier for lunch. "How about the Albright?" she asked. "In the mood for some great seafood?"

"Sure. Sounds good."

Once we were seated and the staff had appropriately fawned over her, my opened menu provided me some respite from having to look at or converse with her.

I just didn't like her. And it wasn't even totally about the fact that she'd been my father's mistress or whatever. It was more than that. She was fake, phony, and couldn't be trusted, of that I was sure. But I knew that I had to at least try with her or this lunch would drag out to eternity, or so it would seem.

I ordered fish tacos, and Tiffany ordered a watercress and shrimp salad.

"So," I said, breaking the uncomfortable silence that always seemed to permeate the space between us, "is that actor—Julian is it? Is he really going to be cut from the show?" I figured I couldn't go wrong picking a favorite subject of Tiffany's: her show.

"Well, I can share this with you I guess, since we're family, but you have to keep it an absolute secret," she whispered, leaning in closer.

"Who would I tell?" I asked, clearly puzzled that she'd even toss that in there.

"You can't tell your school friends, promise?"

I made the 'cross my heart' gesture for her benefit since she seemed to be under the impression that I had school friends, although I wasn't sure how she could have possibly arrived at that conclusion. I chuckled over that, not over her cutesy attempt at sharing a studio secret with me.

"Okay, so it appears that Julian Weatherford will be replaced next season when his character on the show, Austin, comes out of the coma. Studios have run into these types of contract disputes like...forever. So they aren't about to give in to his cheesy agent's salary demands. I mean, the boy thinks he needs to make the same amount per episode as I do, isn't that totally insane?"

Hell, I didn't know what she made per episode, nor did I care. I wasn't in a position to have an opinion one way or another as to the insanity of it. But I nodded so that she would continue to talk and I didn't have to do more than half-listen.

"Well, the producers are holding secret auditions before February sweeps because they're fairly certain they're going to replace Julian after this season. I mean once an actor starts his own star trip like that, it's usually time to part ways."

"Well, that sounds smart," I replied, taking a sip of my iced tea. "Wouldn't want to put all your eggs in one basket I guess."

"Exactly," she said, nodding vehemently. "This show makes too much revenue to let some pimply-faced teenager throw a wrench into it. We have loyal sponsors and a great time slot at risk if we lose them. Why some of them have been with us the whole six seasons we've been on the air."

She waited for me to say something. I guess it was my turn to speak. My mind rushed through everything she'd just said.

"So," I started, "does Julian really have pimples?"

Tiffany's eyes widened and then she giggled yet again. "No, of course not, silly! That's just a saying. He's really handsome.

Dark good looks. But, he's nineteen and thinks he's got the world in his pocket. Time for a wake-up call for his ego. That's the problem with the young talent; so many times their physical appearance tops their level of maturity. They can and often are their own worst enemy in this business. Especially a child star turned heart throb like Julian."

I laughed, drawing a look from my stepmother. "Oh, I was just thinking that you talk like you're old, Tiffany. And clearly you're not."

"Why thank you, Neely," she gushed as if I'd just given her some spectacular compliment. I was simply stating facts here. Yeah, nineteen was young, but so was twenty-nine, which was her age. "But in this business I can tell you that women seem to age much quicker than men. I count my blessings in landing this show, and the opportunities it will provide for other things."

"Other things?"

"Oh sure. Every actor that doesn't say they dream of doing a feature film some day is a damn liar. It's only a matter of time until my ship comes in."

We finally got through lunch and headed home. Tiffany continued to babble on about her show, and the cast, and then, as we passed the Drake home, she suddenly punched the brakes of her Audi and yelled out, "That's it!"

My head snapped back up from the shock of her sudden stop, "What the hell?" I yelled, looking over at her, and rubbing my neck. "You just gave me whiplash!"

"Oh, Neely, I'm sorry hun. I just saw that house and it dawned on me who would be absolutely perfect to audition for the role of Austin Benedict! Seth Drake. He would be amazing for that role."

A flood of panic infiltrated every nerve ending in my body. "You're not *stopping* here, are you?"

She relaxed back and pressed down on the accelerator once again, heading down the road to our house. "No, no. They're in Aspen right now. But you better believe as soon as we start shooting again in January, I'm gonna put a bug in the producer's ear about him."

As she shut the car off, I decided to take a leap and ask Tiffany what she knew about Seth Drake these days. "So, isn't Seth studying in New York?"

"Yes, but he's with his family over the holidays. If I time this right, the studio could probably get a screen test in for him before he returns to school after winter break."

I nodded and remained silent. Worst move I could've made because it triggered something in Tiffany. Curiosity? Sympathy? Or maybe just her own brand of cruelty.

"Ohh...listen, I'm *sorry* Neely. I totally forgot that you two were an *item* of sorts back in the day. But listen, I'm sure you're over it by now, aren't you? I mean it was just puppy love at that age. We've all been through it."

I wasn't about to give her the satisfaction of thinking I carried some schoolgirl torch for Seth, even though I did and maybe always would. "For the record, I broke up with him, Tiffany. I never gave it another thought."

"Well, see then? No biggie. Come on, let's get these packages in and under the tree. It's almost Christmas!"

Chapter 3

NEW YEAR'S EVE, 1996

The house had been blessedly quiet for the past three days. Thank God my father and Tiffany finally left on their cruise. At last I had peace and quiet, and as big as the house was, when Tiffany was present it seemed to close in on me with no chance for privacy or escape.

I stood in the middle of the floor of my bedroom, the carpet covered entirely in a heavy plastic tarp, and finished painting the one wall that didn't have any windows on it.

White.

But that didn't mean I was trying to make some pure and sterile statement, because clearly, I wasn't. It was painted white for a reason. It was my new canvas. No more corkboard. This wall would display any subject matter I was in the mood to paint, be it still life, landscape, abstract, or impressionist. Anything was possible. Tomorrow it would be dry enough to start on my first painting. I decided it would be an abstract of sin.

Yes, I said sin.

In my mind, I knew what sin looked like. The darkness, the negative energy, the brutal reality, and duplicity of it all. The destructive path it swathed across one person's soul. Yes, I decided 'Sin' would be my first creation on my new art wall. My own personal perception and interpretation of it.

I showered and changed into a pair of jeans and a sweatshirt. The staff had taken the week off to enjoy the holidays with their respective families, and I enjoyed having the whole place to myself. No one muddling around asking me if there was anything I wanted or needed.

I needed nothing.

And what I wanted? Well, what I wanted they weren't in a position to provide. I wanted contentment; I wanted comfort at times too. I wanted to forget that my mama was someone I didn't recognize anymore. Not that I had seen or heard from her over the past few months. Nope. Not a word. I'd sent several letters to her in care of the rehab facility where she currently resided. I had at least talked with my grandmother on the phone several times. Whenever I asked about Mama the most she would say was something cryptic.

Oh, she's doing as well as can be expected, Neilah."

It's just going to take some time. Your mama has a lot of pain and anger she's dealing with right now. Just keep her in your prayers, child."

I thought about Mama a lot. The holidays were a reminder of how things used to be, but certainly not the way they were for us right now. At least not for Mama or me.

Daddy seemed to have gone on with his life just fine, and while I didn't necessarily begrudge him happiness, I'd be lying if I said I didn't feel some resentment. The holidays were so overrated I decided. For me, they were just something to get through on my way to freedom and independence. Then I could choose whether or not I wanted to celebrate them.

The sun was going down as I decided to enjoy the peace and tranquility of the beach. I'd been inside all day, painting and touching up, and it was terrible to let the beautiful and balmy weather of Malibu in December go to waste. Besides that, my father had purchased a high-tech camera for me that came with a half-dozen or so gadgets. And the reason I referred to them as *gadgets* is because I had no clue about all the accessories and trappings of photography.

But, for whatever reason, my father presumed that the artist in me might be compelled to give it a try. And so I would, but no promises.

My new Canon EOS 1X camera was supposed to be top-of-the-line as Daddy mentioned when I unwrapped it on Christmas morning.

I knew I hadn't hid my stunned and confused look, because obviously, I'd never had a need of my own camera before. I painted or sketched things I wanted to remember from my memory.

"Look at this, Neely," he'd said excitedly as I took it from the box, "See, it has something they call Advanced Photo System. This isn't your typical thirty-five millimeter film, it's better. Brand new technology. This baby even has an autofocus that uses a sensor for passive, active, or hybrid subjects..."

He might've well been talking Greek to me for all I could understand of it, but he had pointed out the accessories that were comprised of some special lenses and focusing magnifiers. I had plenty of film, so what the hell? I might as well give it a try. The beach was the perfect place to test it out with its dusk to night lenses he'd explained to me. Who knew, maybe I could get some great panoramic shots for a watercolor painting on my new wall.

The beach was deserted like I knew it would be. It wasn't as if it was ever crowded being that it was private, but the intermittent jogger or couples walking hand-in-hand weren't visible. Most people in the area vacationed somewhere else over the holidays, and that was fine with me.

The temperature was still in the mid-fifties, and a light ocean breeze caressed my cheeks as I spread a blanket down on the sand and sat down to figure this contraption out. I pulled my camera out of my backpack and spent the next twenty minutes getting it prepped. Then I commenced focusing on the sun that was quickly disappearing in a fusion of radiant color behind the seascape.

After awhile, I walked down the beach, catching flocks of seagulls preparing to take cover for the night wherever that might be. About fifty yards ahead I came to the rock pile that had been there for years as a marker for the fishing boats so they'd keep their distance from the shallow reef that existed. Seth and I had spent many an afternoon on the reef, exploring, talking, and skipping stones from the top of the piling. I climbed to the top and sat down. I switched out the lens on my camera to one that supposedly accommodated night photography. I guess I'd find out when I developed the film.

Under the star splattered sky, I took some very still pictures of the ocean waves as they lapped up against the rock formation. There was something very intimate in filming things at night I decided. Somehow, it seemed as if I was invading nature's privacy.

I liked it.

An hour later I started back down the beach. I'd used up two rolls of film. The jury was no longer out on my father's present to me. I'd enjoyed my first venture into photography, and I would definitely be adding it to my list of hobbies.

I had almost reached the steps leading up to our property, when the sound of male laughter drifted up to me just as I'd bent down to gather up my blanket and backpack from the sand.

I immediately straightened up and peered down the beach from where I'd heard the sounds. But the darkness had shrouded visibility to the extent that I couldn't make out more than some moving shadows.

I didn't need to see them to know that one of them was Seth. I recognized his laughter. And then I did one of the most dumbass things possible. But in all fairness, I hadn't really thought it through. I pulled my camera up and turned on the flash in hopes I could unobtrusively shine it in that general direction to see him.

Yeah. Not my best move for sure. But at least I had the presence of mind to duck behind the brush around the staircase before I made that stupid move.

I had no clue the light would be so bright as to catch their attention, but yeah, it was.

I watched as Seth's head snapped up and peered over his shoulder down towards where I hid behind the random branches.

Shit!

I hurriedly clicked the light off, and pulled the strap of my camera over my head to free my hands. I grabbed my backpack, and stepped out from behind the brush and started up the steps. I'd only made it to the first landing before his voice, now deep and rich with masculinity, reached my ears.

"Neely? Neely, wait," he ordered. "Don't run away from me."

I stopped immediately in my tracks, but made no move to turn around just yet.

Run away?

I don't run away, do I?

And I knew the answer to that question almost immediately. Yes. Running was in fact what I had done two years prior. I ran from Seth, but whether that was the right thing to do or not seemed inconsequential now. He hadn't seemed to mind after all. I'd never heard from him again.

I hadn't been the *bad guy* in any of it. I had no reason to second-guess that decision. What was done was done. I had no compunction to feel ashamed or apologetic even because, after all, how much had Seth Drake really cared?

My shoulders relaxed as I dropped my backpack onto the landing and turned around to face him. After two freakin' years, I was face-to-face once again with Seth Drake. And no matter how I justified the past in my mind, I was still terrified.

Chapter 4

July 23, 1994

> *Two and a half years prior*

Our lips were melded together, Seth's warm breath and scent seemed to be part of me now as his tongue explored my mouth and we struck some sort of a cadence that put us in sync. The windows in his car were fogged up, giving us some privacy.

We were parked in our favorite spot, just down the highway from Malibu in a park preserve that was all but deserted. One dirt road that went off from the main paved one, led into the wooded area that sheltered us from view.

His hands had moved lower, his fingers tracing over my belly and then dipping beneath the waistband of my shorts.

I should stop him.

This was where I usually stopped him, but my body was sending off a completely different vibe.

Seth's mouth continued to work mine with gentle precision, and my tongue danced with his in anticipation of how far we would take this, though I knew in my mind, that the decision was mine.

My heart raced as Seth's fingers gently probed beneath my panties. I felt my breath hitch, and an audible gasp escaped my lips when I felt him dip a finger inside of me. I froze.

His lips were still against mine, and I felt his words when he whispered, "Relax, baby. Just go with it. Trust me, please?"

I relaxed beneath him and we resumed our frenzied kissing. I could almost hear the pounding of my heart, and my mind was full of confettied thoughts, mere bits and pieces all over the place, and in total conflict with one another.

On one hand, I had this innate need to please Seth, and to trust him as he requested. I loved him. I wanted us to be physical with one another, but not just yet. Not when I would be hauling my ass back to Tennessee in a couple of weeks and what then?

Those conflicted thoughts clouded my mind and, momentarily, shut out the here and now, but not for long.

Seth's fingers were working magic with my flesh, both inside and out. His lips were now teasing my nipples, in a very delicious way. And my body was responding in *every* way. I felt my pelvis thrust up against his hand, not once or twice, but many times. I realized it was an instinctual move; my body's response to the pleasure I was feeling deep within.

Warm tingling sensations had brought a fevered dampness to my sensitive folds, and when Seth's thumb rotated slowly on the fleshy nub that seemed to have become engorged on its own, I felt the heat within me rising to an unfamiliar pitch. My hands clutched his hair and my body convulsed in involuntary spasms as shock waves of pure pleasure coursed through every inch of it. I gasped audibly at the intensity of the throbbing pleasure as it slowly subsided within me.

"Oh my God," I breathed out finally, my limbs now starting to relax; the tingling sensation was ebbing and, in its place, I was overwhelmed with a sense of calm satisfaction.

"Seth," I gasped, my voice held a raspy tremor, and my hands grasped his head, urging him up and off of me, "we need to take it down a notch. I think we went too far just now."

He scooted up and over to his seat, and I couldn't miss the bulge in his jeans, and then he chuckled. "I think it's too late for that, Neely. Unless you think orgasms come with a return policy."

My cheeks reddened as I quickly moved to put my clothes back in place. "Is...is that what that was?" I asked, my eyes were wide with curiosity.

"Well yeah, silly. Don't tell me you don't know about orgasms, because I know you read Cosmo. Saw it on our blanket at the beach the other day," he said with a snicker.

I rolled my eyes at him. "Of course I know what they are. Well in *theory*, I mean."

He laughed again as he adjusted his crotch unabashedly, "Now you know *in reality* I guess."

I ran a hand through my hair, and then turned to him, "Seth, I'm just not ready for you know...the *full Monty*."

And to my surprise, Seth broke out into raucous laughter. So not what I had expected.

"The *full Monty*?" he asked, his eyes twinkled with amusement. "Are you serious, Neely?"

I crossed my arms and shot him a dirty look. "It's British slang for your information, Seth! It's just an idiom, you know, like...*the whole enchilada*, or *the whole nine yards*?"

My explanation only served to illicit more of his deep, rich laughter into the situation. "Stop...Neely! You're killin' me here, girl...*enchilada...nine yards*?" He repeated, now holding his stomach as he continued to be highly amused at my expense.

Now I was pissed. "I'm so fucking glad I kept you entertained, Seth, at least your hard-on's gone."

He immediately did his best to compose himself, and gave me a frown. "Okay, okay—sorry, but I'm not laughing at you, I'm laughing at me. You see, when you said that," he started, with an involuntary chuckle, "I thought you were giving a name to my...well, to my dick."

"Huh?" It was my turn to be amused I guess.

Now his cheeks colored a bit and he chewed on a fingernail. "Yeah, you know, I guess some girls do that with their boyfriends. They give pet names to the guy's dick, and the guy gives a pet name to the girl's—"

"Stop!" I hollered, my hand reached over and clamped his mouth shut, "Please do not finish that thought, Seth," I replied, but I couldn't help smiling at the absurdity of it nonetheless. Who would actually name one another's privates?

"So," he said, his hand taking mine away from his mouth and pressing it into his. "Are you saying you don't want to name my cock, Monty?" he chuckled. "Hey, how about we make his last name *Python*?"

And then we both busted out laughing, and finally, the intensity of only moments ago vanished and once again we were Neely and Seth, boyfriend and girlfriend...at least for now.

"Can I think about it?" I asked slyly, not wanting to get back on the subject of body parts at the moment.

"I hope you do," he replied, his tone had shifted back to serious, "But more than that, I want you to think about how much I want to make love to you, Neely. Damn, I think about you all the time. And usually, when I do, Monty comes to the party if you know what I mean."

I flushed at his admission, and I knew exactly what he meant. And the truth was, I wanted what he wanted too...*physically* that is. But I knew once that step was taken, it would change things emotionally and that was the part that scared the hell out of me. I didn't want to be that lovesick girl planted two thousand miles away, replaying moments with Seth over and over in my mind as some sort of consolation prize because it was all I had.

"Seth," I replied softly, "I love you. I want to be with you more than anything, but I'm scared."

He raised the palm of my hand to his lips and spread soft kisses all over it. "Baby, there's nothing to be scared of, I promise. I will be as gentle as possible with you—I don't want it to be painful, trust me."

I smiled. "It's not that, Seth. I'm not scared of the physical part of it."

He raised a brow quizzically. "Then what, Neely? What scares you?"

I turned my face to gaze out of the window so that he couldn't read all the insecurities that resided in my head. "I'm afraid that it won't solve anything, and in fact, that it will only make it all the more complicated for us. I don't want it to be the first time Seth and Neely had sex with each other. I want it to be the first of many times in their lives together that Seth and Neely made love."

I turned back around to catch his reaction. He was thoughtful, almost brooding at the moment. Finally he spoke, "So, what? You think this will mean nothing to me? You have my promise ring, Neely. It means that we're together. But shit, we're teenagers here—way too young for a lifetime commitment, don't you think?"

"Of course I do," I replied, "And that's the problem I guess. I don't want to take this step when we're both so young. It might be different if I still lived down the road. We'd be going into adulthood together, seeing if our relationship could and would survive the growth and transition that's all a part of living. I don't want to have regrets—not where you're concerned."

He moaned in frustration. That wasn't what he wanted to hear from me. I suspected he wasn't going to drop the subject easily. Seth was stubborn. I was stubborn. This could go either way.

"Look," he said, releasing a hard sigh, and squeezing my hand tightly, "I want to be with you. I made a promise to you, and I thought that meant something. I'm not going to pressure you anymore than I already have, that just wouldn't be cool."

I relaxed visibly, but I knew there was more coming.

"But," he continued, his blue eyes piercing a hole through my heart, "I want you to think about it. Tomorrow I have a late rehearsal, but after that, I'm all yours, baby. And I hope that you'll be all mine too."

After that he'd driven me home, and with the parting kiss at my door, I knew that Seth was determined to have the *full Monty*. But the question that was looming in my mind all that night was whether I was prepared to deliver.

Chapter 5

My eyes swept over him surreptitiously. I could see that Seth had matured physically, and I was fucking impressed.

Taller than even two and a half years prior, he had to be six-one, maybe six-two. He was muscular and tanned; his hair was a bit longer I could tell, even as it fringed out beneath the ball cap he had perched on his head backwards.

But those eyes.

Even in the darkness the blue was radiant. He looked like a fucking rock star and he wore that look well.

"I wasn't running away," I finally sputtered, "I was just going up to my house."

"Ah," he replied, cockily, eyeing me with no reservation. Most likely he was taking the same physical inventory with his blue orbs that I'd just taken with my brown ones. I wondered how I measured up in Seth's eyes.

I was five feet four and a half, and had been for the past year, so I didn't think I'd be getting any taller than that anytime soon. I was slender, and my dark blonde hair fell well past my shoulders. I'd been thinking about going blonder, but up to this point, I'd not taken that step.

"Looks like you filled out some," was his remark. "You look good."

"Ditto," I replied, my teeth tugging at my bottom lip as my pulse quickened. What was left to say here?

"You staying here by yourself?" he asked, nodding up towards the yard where our house sat.

"Yep. Dad's on a cruise with the wife. I thought your family was in Aspen?" I immediately regretted the last remark because, well, *because* it made it obvious that I somehow knew their business, or more accurately, *his* business.

"Got back yesterday. You know Laura and Kent with their New Year's Eve parties. It's a tradition with them."

I laughed lightly.

That was a fact.

I remembered the years I had lived here that every New Year's Eve the Drakes would host a big party. Mama and Daddy had even gone on a couple occasions. When we were younger, they made sure one of the staff kept the children entertained with rented movies, pizzas and soda, and out of the hair of the adults who were there for one purpose and one purpose only: to party until at least some of them puked.

"What are you thinking about, Tennessee?" he asked softly, bringing me back to the present.

It seemed perfectly natural in that second to hear him call me "Tennessee." So natural, that I didn't even hesitate before answering. "Just thinking about the parties your folks had when mine came over, and how we used to spy on some of the celebrities that got totally wasted. Too bad I didn't have this camera then," I finished, tapping the one that hung around my neck.

Seth chuckled too. "No shit. You could've sold some of them for major bucks. Neighborhood paparazzi, right?"

I nodded but remained silent. That word. *Paparazzi.* It held some major negative vibes for me and I guess it always would. But for that, my parents might still be together this day. But deep down, I knew that wasn't the truth. It might have expedited the split, but I was old enough now to see the truth. Their split was inevitable. They'd outgrown one another; they had different dreams. It happened. No sense in dwelling on the past.

"So, pretty nifty camera you've got there. You taking up a different hobby?" he asked.

"Just a new one," I replied, and deep within me my heart ached to tell him all about the photos I'd taken this evening.

Sharing.

It was one of the things Seth and I had done.

A million years ago.

He nodded, and started to say something more when someone from down on the beach hollered up to us. "Seth! Dude! Come on! Need to get some more refreshments down here. What the hell kind of party is this, man?"

"I'm coming, Jack!" he hollered back, "Chill your shit, man!"

He turned back to me. "Hey, well it's been nice seeing you, Neely. I got a party to get back to. You living back here now or just visiting?"

So, he didn't know.

I was sure Laura had seen me breeze by on more than one occasion, though I made it a point not to look over when I drove past. I just felt funny about everything.

"Living here," I replied. "Since September. Do you like New York?"

"Ah, yeah, New York is badass. I go back on the tenth. Can hardly wait."

He stepped back and shoved his hands into the pocket of his cargo pants, "Well, I gotta jet, Neely. Take care."

As he turned to leave, something inside of me screamed to not let him leave without hearing something more from me. "Seth," I called out, "About the letter—"

His face contorted into something that resembled pure anger, though since I'd never seen Seth angry, I couldn't be sure of it. "Don't," he snapped, and then calmed immediately. "Don't give it another thought, Tennessee. I haven't. Our lives are both good, yeah?"

I nodded slowly. Even though it wasn't quite true for me.

"Then that's all that fucking matters."

And then he was gone.

Chapter 6

It was just after midnight when I was awakened by a loud pounding on our front door, along with the intermittent ringing of the doorbell.

What the hell?

I jumped from my bed and padded down the hallway and into the large entrance hall where I could see someone standing out front in the cut glass side views. I peered through one of them and gasped in surprise.

It was Seth.

As soon as I opened the door, I could see it was an inebriated Seth. I was stunned by the fact that he was standing there with what looked like a bottle of champagne dangling in one hand, and a shit-eating grin on his face.

"Seth?" I said, my sleepy confusion was apparent.

"Yeah, Neely, it's me. Happy Fucking New Year!" he shouted, taking the open door as an invitation for him to sweep inside the house as if he were invited. "Let's toast 1997, babe. This is some freaking Dom Perignon I snagged from the party. Where're your champagne glasses?"

I was still dealing with the fact that he'd left his friends to come over here. "Wait. What?"

"It's *champagne*. It's what people drink to toast the New Year in, okay?"

His eyes were doing a bugging out thing that quite frankly, I didn't care for one little bit. It was if he thought I was some back woods hillbilly that didn't comprehend the whole toasting thing on New Year's Eve, and hell no, I didn't appreciate that shit one bit.

"Now you just wait one damn minute, Seth Drake! You don't come over to my house in the dead of night to treat me like some ignorant hill jack, got it?"

He smirked, cocking his head a bit. "Yeah, Tennessee, I got it. Didn't mean to be an ass," he relented, giving me his crooked grin. "So, how about it? Will you have a glass of champagne with me?"

"Well, maybe just one," I conceded, heading into the dining room to get the glasses.

My one glass of champagne turned into three, but Seth was way ahead of me in that regard. I noticed he hadn't finished his first glass yet. Had that been his plan?

"So," I said, "Is the party over at your house? Is that why you're here?"

"Nooo," he said softly, taking the glass from me and placing it on the coffee table. "That's not why I'm here, Neely."

My skin prickled with goose bumps as his eyes assessed me brazenly. I was wearing the pink silk nightie that Tiffany had given me for Christmas. And by the way Seth was perusing me, I might as well have been sitting next to him naked. "Why *are* you here?"

He shrugged. "Not sure. I just felt like our conversation earlier was cut short, I guess. A lot of things were left unsaid."

I shifted, tucking a leg underneath me and turned my body towards him on the sofa. "Listen, Seth, about what I wrote—"

"No, Neely," he cut in, "I don't want to talk about that damn letter. Not now or ever. I want to talk about how beautiful you looked when I first saw you again. Tonight on the beach. The moon and the stars as your backdrop. Just you and me in the darkness. It felt…I don't know how to explain it…it felt *surreal*. I guess I never figured I see you again. That you'd never come back here for any reason."

It struck me as odd that Seth had given it so much thought, one way or the other, but the fact he'd just said as much, made me feel a bit giddy. Or maybe the champagne was just kicking in, either way, I felt giddy and warm.

He was watching me. It was my turn to say something I realized. "So much has happened, Seth. I don't even know where to start."

"How about we start right here?"

Before I could process the meaning of his words, his lips crashed down upon mine with a passionate hunger that took me by surprise. In the same moment, his body pressed against mine, his weight pinning me against the couch pillows. I finally was able to struggle free from him.

"Seth—Seth, wait."

He pulled back; his voice was now husky with need. "I don't want to wait for you a minute longer, Neely. Don't you understand? I feel like I've been waiting a lifetime to be with you, to make love to you, to be inside of you. Are you going to deny me this? Tell me to go, and I swear to God, I'll go. Tell me, Neely, tell me to walk out that goddamned door and I'm gone. Say those words to me."

But I couldn't say those words. If I said those words to him they would all be a lie and I knew it. My heart knew it, and my soul was sure of it.

"No. I don't want you to go, Seth. I want you to stay."

I stood up from the sofa, and held my hand out for him to take. He did, rising up to stand next to me. His eyes peered down at me, and I could tell that my words registered by the quiet calm in his face.

For a moment we just stood there, face to face, gazing into one another's eyes for the truth. I knew he could see mine, but when I looked into his blue eyes, I was having trouble reading his. It wasn't like me to not be able to read Seth's emotions, but then again, a lot might've changed over the past couple of years.

So, I did the responsible thing. I broke the silence with four simple words: "Do you have protection?"

Chapter 7

We were in my bedroom, lying buck naked on my bed, with nothing but votive candles lit on my dresser. Tiffany had insisted the staff distribute Christmas scented votives all throughout the house for the holidays. Right now they served up a sensual tone rather than a festive one.

Chalk one up for ole Tiffany I thought to myself as I admired Seth's body. He didn't seem to mind. "Like what you see, Neely?"

And that caused me to blush, because yeah, I'd been pretty obvious about eye fucking him. But then, I was a virgin so this was a pretty big deal for me. I wasn't about to go into this with my eyes wide shut and miss it all. I was an artist, and a 'maybe' photographer some day, so everything was a visual opportunity from my perspective. Maybe it would even inspire an awesome element for my "Sin" montage.

"Second thoughts?" Seth whispered as he turned on his side and ran his fingers slowly along the swell of my breasts. He moved his face to my neck, and allowed his tongue to gently trace a path along my collarbone. I shivered, and rose to my knees, my body now faced his as he reclined on his side, his chin now perched on the knuckles of his right hand.

"No, but you need to know something, Seth. This will be my first time, and I make no apologies for my lack of sexual expertise."

There. I had put it out there. No mincing words for me, because that wasn't my style and Seth knew it.

He drew up from his reclined position, and scooted closer to me. One hand cupped my chin and he tilted my face upward. His gaze penetrated mine and, for a second, I saw a flicker of something pass over his face.

Was it surprise? Did he simply presume that I'd replaced him with someone else, or that I could have even done that so easily?

Doubt? But why would he doubt me? Did he really think two years had changed me into someone who regarded sex with casual nonchalance?

Indecision? Was he having second thoughts now?

Whatever it was, it was gone in a flash. He lowered his lips to mine and kissed them softly. "Whatever you say, baby."

And then I looped my arms around his neck to pull him even closer because this was Seth. And for this moment, he was mine again. I wanted him to claim me, to make me his again. I craved our lost connection. I wanted the time and distance that had come between us to be irrevocably removed, if not forever, then at least for now.

Our naked bodies were now pressed against one another, and I felt his bold erection between us. I gasped just a little.

Seth pulled one of my arms from around his neck, and moved my hand downward between us, placing my hand where he wanted it. I closed my fingers around his erection, not sure just how careful I needed to be when handling it.

He must've sensed my apprehension. "Monty won't break, Neely. I'll let you know if you get too rough, don't worry."

And I immediately felt more at ease, smiling against his lips at the reference to "Monty."

He remembered.

I refused to allow thoughts of Seth being with other girls over the past couple of years invade my thoughts. It was none of my business. He'd had every right to move on after I'd left the note for him. I didn't want to know. I only wanted now.

Seth pressed me back against the mattress so that I was now flat on my back. His eyes flickered over my body, taking in every inch of it with his hungry gaze.

I did the same with him. His sculpted body mesmerized me. Corded muscles, flat abs, broad chest, strong shoulders, and a chiseled face with just enough five o'clock shadow present to make him look a bit older than his nineteen years.

Artists appreciate perfection in every subject matter, and Seth Drake was masculine perfection personified. There was no doubt in my artist's mind, or from my perspective as a woman. A woman who right now wanted to feel every part of him with her own hands.

So, that's what I did. I reached up, letting my hands graze across his powerful thighs slowly and languidly as he straddled me. I explored his manhood tentatively, my fingers testing the flesh in amazement at the different textures of skin. Velvety soft in places, hard muscled and rigid elsewhere.

He drew in a ragged breath as I continued to stroke him. But like I told him at the start, I wasn't well-versed by any means in the art of pleasuring a guy. I was going by instinct, something I was sure Cosmo would frown upon.

Seth abruptly changed his position, causing my hand to release him, and spread my thighs with his knees as he now took his place between them.

He crouched over me, his mouth hot and wet, covered a breast and soon his tongue circled the nipple. But he wasn't going to linger there for long. He moved his attention lower, his lips skimmed my belly and then moved down even further.

I gasped as I felt his lips and tongue invade my folds masterfully, my knuckles blanched as I gripped the bottom sheet tightly with my fingers, allowing a soft moan to escape on my next exhaled breath. I could not only hear the wetness, I could feel it between my thighs as Seth made soft sweet love to me with his mouth and tongue.

"Please!" I pleaded, my body now consumed with this innate need to feel his fullness inside of me.

Seth straightened up and grabbed the condom he'd placed on my nightstand when we'd first arrived in my room.

With his eyes boring into mine, he ripped the corner with his teeth, and extracted the condom. In one swift motion, he rolled the latex onto his length, and my mind registered the fact that he did this with practiced precision.

Don't go there, Neely.

He now hovered over me, resting his weight upon his arms braced on either side of me. I felt his warm breath caress my cheek as he whispered huskily, "Are you ready, Neely?"

I nodded quickly. Better to have the first part over with as quickly as possible and replace the pain with pleasure I decided.

Seth's lips met mine as he guided himself with one hand, and then pressed himself inside of me in one, swift and deliberate thrust. I felt a sharp stab of flashing pain and despite my resolve not to, I groaned. Seth stilled immediately. I could feel the thunderous beating of his heart against my own. I sucked in a deep breath, wondering if that was as bad as it would get.

"You okay?" he murmured gently, his lips placing soft kisses along my jaw line. "Want me to stop?"

"No," I answered quickly. "I think the worst is over."

He then slowly and methodically moved inside of me. The pain started to ebb and I realized that I wasn't split in half. I had survived the desecration of my hymen with everything else intact. And now I wanted more.

I wrapped my legs around his hips firmly, and allowed my body to pull him inside deeper. That was my body's signal to Seth that all systems were go.

With our bodies firmly entwined, Seth continued to move and thrust within me. The uncomfortable tightness was quickly replaced with my own body's instinctual need for sexual pleasuring.

I moved against him, meeting him thrust for thrust. And when his tempo increased, my body arched up against his until the budding, splintering feeling of having our bodies fused together released the most ecstatic sensations I've ever known. It was as if my core had its own pulse as wave after wave of pleasure was released from deep within. I didn't even try to stifle the primal moans that spilled from my lips, and at the apex of it all, I cried out his name over and over again.

When he relaxed against me, our breathing was still coming fast and hard. His lips found their way to mine, and I kissed him so hard and fiercely it surprised even me.

"Seth," I gasped. "I fucking love you." And I continued to pepper his face and neck with kisses because I knew what I had said just now was the only truth, and it always had been the truth for me.

Chapter 8

When I awoke the following morning, I stretched languidly beneath the covers, and then turned to my side.

The bed was empty.

I sat up abruptly, brushing my hair back off of my face and looked around the room. Seth was gone. All signs of him being here were gone as well, I realized as I dropped my feet to the carpeted floor and peered around the bed.

Used condoms gone.

Condom wrappers gone.

Seth gone.

I pulled the covers back, as if I actually believed he was crouched down beneath the sheets, blanket, comforter, and bed pillows hiding from me. All that I saw were several blood stains, proof of what had transpired last night hadn't been a seductive dream on my part.

I felt my forehead crease in confusion. Seth and I had enjoyed several rounds of lovemaking, and each time seemed to surpass the time before in the intensity of orgasmic pleasure, well, at least from my perspective. I couldn't speak for him, but it sure as hell seemed as if he enjoyed himself plenty.

We'd fallen asleep with me curled against him, his arm thrown over me protectively. I racked my brain to recall what had been said between us before we'd drifted off to sleep, fully spent from our sexual activities.

Then I remembered. He'd said something about having some friends come by this evening to have a New Year's Day cookout on the beach. He wanted me to come down and join them. I hadn't acted enthused about it, particularly since I wouldn't know a soul except for him.

But Seth, with his power of persuasion, had convinced me that they were all chill people and to give them a chance. I'd eventually capitulated when his tongue had teased me in a very special place that seemed to turn me into mindless jelly whenever he visited the region.

So, I was committed to going. Casual dress he said. Seven o'clock on the beach. I was to be there or be square according to Seth.

I spent the day fretting about the beach party. I wasn't an overly social person, and he knew that. I couldn't understand why this damn cookout was so important on his list of things to do on New Year's Day. I could've come up with plenty more activities that wouldn't have taken us out of this bedroom.

I laughed to myself. One night of sex and suddenly I'd transitioned into some horny teenager. Well, it wasn't as if I had the urge to be with other guys, no, that definitely wasn't what I needed. I only ever wanted to be with Seth, and my hopes were that he felt the same way.

Yeah, I got that we were both so young with massive growing up to do, but what was wrong with doing that together? After all, I was back in California. I knew what his dreams were and California provided the perfect landscape for that. My dreams could be pursued just about anywhere.

But the problem was, that Seth and I hadn't done much talking last night. Our bodies had communicated very nicely, but I really hoped to get the chance to have a long, one-on-one conversation with him before he went back to New York in a few days. We had a ton of catching up to do, and I needed to explain why I'd run off the way I had without throwing his mother under the bus.

It was nearly seven-thirty before I'd finally summoned the nerve to head down to the beach for Seth's get together. Nothing wrong with being fashionably late, but really, in L.A. nobody was ever on time. Of course, I didn't have 'the 401' to blame.

I'd spent a good part of the afternoon pampering myself with a long bubble bath, and giving myself a facial with some high-end machine that Tiffany had in her bathing suite. I'd watched her use it before so I decided why the hell not.

I'd done my nails and even managed to get my hair pulled back in a perfect French braid (on the third attempt). I had then fretted over what to wear since Seth's friends were going to be there and I'd already be at a disadvantage by being the only stranger in the group. I finally decided on the fourth or fifth sweater I'd tried on from my Christmas stash. I went through my closet for a clean pair of jeans.

I hated the fact that with a perfectly good laundry suite in the house, and yes, everything was called a *suite* out here, Tiffany still insisted on sending all of the laundry out with a service.

Every third day the service sent their van to pick up the dirty laundry, and the next day it all came back washed, starched, ironed, and folded. Who the hell ever heard of that for jeans, tees, and underwear?

I pulled a pair of my more worn jeans from beneath the plastic wrap that enshrouded them on a hanger. I tried my best to scrunch them up and make them look less starched, but I wasn't making much progress and I was already late. I finally pulled them on and did a few squats to loosen them up. That was about as good as it was going to get. No more procrastinating I told myself.

Let's do this.

It was pretty dark as I made my way down the steps from my yard to the beach. The night was clear, plenty of stars were out, and the moon was full.

Down the beach, I could see the glow of the bonfire going. Several people were milling about, and as I got closer, I could make out Seth's profile. My heart immediately skipped a few beats, and I felt downright nervous as I approached the group.

Seth spotted me as I got closer. "Hey, there she is," he called out. "Thought maybe you were going to bug out on us tonight, Neely," he said, giving me a crooked grin.

"No such luck, Seth," I replied smiling.

He approached me, and put an arm around my shoulders, leading me closer to where three other guys were sitting cross-legged on blankets, poking at the fire and swigging beer from cans.

"Guys," Seth announced, getting their attention, "This is Neely Evans. She lives down the beach, and has recently returned to Cali from Tennessee. Neely, from left to right, these bums are Jack Davis, Nelson Snyder, and Blake McMillan. I met them "in the business," so to speak."

Each of the guys jumped to their feet, brushing sand from their hands to shake mine. "Hey Neely," Jack said giving me a warm smile, "Welcome to our nightmare on the beach." He followed it with an evil laugh, which led me to believe Jack was pursuing his talents in shock theatre. "Hi Jack," I greeted, taking in his dark good looks. Almost as hot as Seth, but not quite.

"Yo, home girl," Nelson said, flipping up some kind of a gang sign, and then laughing and pulling me in for a hug. "Hi Nelson," I giggled, pulling back to study his features. Red hair, lots of tats, and cool as fuck. I liked him.

"Nelson's a goof as you can tell," Seth said from behind me.

I turned to the third one. He was the tallest of the group, sandy blonde hair, which was worn a bit longer than the others, and he had very soft, delicate features. I'd peg him in a minute to know every play Shakespeare had written by heart. "M'lady," Blake greeted, kissing my hand, "What fairest Demoiselle doth grace our meager fare with her beauty?"

"And Blake would be goofier," Seth said with a chuckle.

I pulled my hand from his, and smiled. "You are overly kind, good sir, but I fear such flattery might warp my senses," I replied, giving him some of his own.

Blake threw back his head and laughed in delight. "Touché, Neely. Are you in theatre as well?" he asked, clearly interested.

"She's in high school, *dumbass*," Seth retorted, "Neely's an artist."

I turned to glance up at Seth, confused by his obvious irritation with Blake for the question, and the fact that he'd wasted no time in branding me as a high schooler in front of his buddies. I was only a grade behind him, so why was it such a big deal? His face remained expressionless.

"An artist, huh?" Blake asked, ignoring Seth's remark and taking my arm, "Come then, sit over here, and tell me about your passion. Wanna beer?"

"Thanks, I'm good," I replied, looking back over my shoulder at Seth who was simply looking after us with a dark scowl on his face. None of this seemed familiar.

Not this crowd, certainly not Seth, or the way he was acting. Why had he invited me here if my presence seemed to irritate him?

Blake took a seat and patted the blanket beside him. "Take a load off, Neely. I want to hear about your art."

I sat down cross-legged and gazed over at him. "Why?"

He laughed, "Now that's a dumb question. Okay, why not? It's your passion, right? We all have our passions, you got a hint of mine. I'm studying Medieval Theatre at UCLA. Second year. By the way, I met Seth last summer at an actor's workshop. I've been a sticky booger he can't shake ever since. Dude's brilliant, that's for damn sure."

"Is he?" I asked, clearly interested. That was a part of Seth I had never known. While he'd spent plenty of time watching over my shoulder while I sketched something or painted a landscape, I'd never been privy to his acting abilities. It's not that I wouldn't have been interested, because clearly, I would have, but the extent he shared it with me was in the abstract.

"I wanna be a famous actor some day, Neely. I want to be on television and eventually, I want to be in movies. I think it'd be so cool to play different parts, you know? Be the bad guy sometimes, and then play a hero or two so people could see my diversity? I know I'd be damn good at it, because Laura says I'm a born natural."

"Oh absolutely," Blake continued. "He blew me away last summer. He's into that whole Stella Adler technique of acting. Works well for him, too."

I was lost. "What's the Stella Adler technique?"

Blake explained that unlike method acting, the Adler technique took it much further than that. "It's not playing a part per se, that can come off as faking it, you know? It's kind of complicated, but the best way to explain it is that the actor uses his imagination to create specific images in the mind—images with him actually living the part, not just acting it. So in effect, he is surrounding himself with those mental images. That way, the actor is being true to himself in character, and won't have to lie or be fake in front of the camera."

I nodded, but it still seemed so abstract to me. What kind of images I wondered, but I felt stupid asking. "So in a way, in a particular role, the actor is fully invested not only in the character, but with everything else around him?"

"Bingo!" Blake said, "By George, I think you've got it!"

I giggled. "Sounds complicated to me, but I know it's been Seth's dream for like forever."

"Now your turn. I've been waiting."

What I did seemed so lame after hearing about Seth and his brilliant acting abilities, but I was always happy to talk about my art. I shared with Blake some of the media and subject matter I preferred, and where I hoped to go with it after graduation. "It's easier to show than explain I guess. I just know that it's something I've loved doing since I was little. Started with finger painting all over Mama's living room walls back in Tennessee."

He laughed and then stopped abruptly, "Hey, did you do that piece hanging up in Seth's bedroom?" he asked.

I was a tad stunned that it was still there. "Um...yeah, you saw it?"

"Hell yeah. Hard to miss. It's brilliant by the way, but then, I'm no expert with art, just know what I like."

"Thanks," I replied, looking around to see where Seth was at the moment.

He was drinking a beer, talking to Jack and Nelson. Again, I wondered why he'd invited me here if his plan was to ignore me. Now I was getting a little pissed, but I sure as hell wasn't going to make the first move to be social with the host.

"Aha," I heard Blake say from behind me now. He'd stood up. "Here come the bimbos."

I whirled back around and watched as four girls, all looking to be around eighteen or nineteen descended the wooden steps from Seth's backyard to the beach.

"Excuse me?" I said, looking at Blake. "The bimbos?"

He chuckled good naturedly, giving me a gentle smack on the back. "Don't take offense, Neely, they know I call them that and like me anyway. By the way, they're gonna love that sweet little Southern accent of yours. Don't get stung."

My forehead creased in confusion, but Blake had already started walking towards them. "Thank fuck! Let's eat, Drake!"

Chapter 9

Why the hell was I here?

No, the better question was: Why in the hell had I *stayed* here after the bimbos had arrived? Was I clueless?

The *bimbos*, as it turned out, were the *girlfriends*. That's right. Four girls. Four guys. And then there was me. Apparently, I was the entertainment.

I wasn't about to give Seth the satisfaction of thinking I was bothered by any of it. After all, he'd gone to so much trouble getting me down here. I certainly didn't want his efforts to be wasted, now did I?

Brought champagne to me. √

Seduced me with kisses. √

Took my virginity. √

Invited me over to meet his girlfriend. √√

I'd gone over to where Seth was busy loading up the grill with burgers and brats for the introductions.

"Hey, Neely," Blake started, putting his arm around a very petite and very pretty black girl, "This is Jasmine Moon."

She smiled brightly and genuinely, holding out her hand for me to shake. "Please, call me Jazzy," she said, "And it's great to finally meet you, Neely. Having a good holiday?"

Her statement momentarily confused me. Had Seth talked about me to his friends? Good sign I decided.

"Nice meeting you, Jazzy—and yes, it's uh...definitely been one to remember."

Jack spoke up, his arm around another blonde girl, shorter in stature and immediately I could tell she was the quiet shy type. She curled into him as if she were afraid the others might devour her. "Neely, this is Amy. Amy, this is Neely."

"Hi Neely," the girl said timidly, "glad to meet you."

"You too, Amy."

"And this, is Julia," Nelson said, smacking a blonde girl around my height and build on the butt. "Neely moved back here from Tennessee," he added, "She's our home girl, dig it."

"Hi, Julia," I said, holding my hand out to her. She acted as if she wasn't sure what she was supposed to do, but finally, she took it in a limp handshake.

"Hey," was all she said before quickly turning to look at the girl with the jet-black hair who was now standing over by the grill. The girl was talking in a low, angry whisper to Seth, whose back was to the rest of us. "Chloe, don't be rude," Julia called out. "Come and meet Neely from Tennessee."

She attached a Southern accent to "Tennessee." Okay, so I could tell at least two of the girls were gonna be bitches. The jury was still out on Jazzy and Amy; but they seemed to be genuine enough. The other two not so much.

Chloe turned around and stalked over to where the rest of us were standing. Her eyes assessed me from top to bottom, finally resting on my face. She didn't appear impressed.

"Yo, I'm Chloe," she announced, "I'm with Seth." Her eyes took on a haughty, I-dare-you-to-say-different attitude, as they continued to bore into mine with casual indifference.

"Chloe," Seth warned from behind her. "Be nice, please?"

If I'd had a stake in my hand at the moment, I would've had no problem in pounding it through Seth's heart. I wondered what smarmy Chloe would say if I told her Seth had spent the better portion of last night and early this morning fucking me silly?

No, I wasn't going to go there. The smile never left my face as I gave her a friendly wink and replied, "Hi there, Chloe, pleased to meet ya!" I said, accentuating my Tennessee accent that I was damn proud of! "Oh, and congrats on that Seth thing."

The guys chuckled, well all accept for Seth who was back manning the grill. Out of my peripheral vision I saw Julia elbow Nelson in the ribs, which resulted in him stifling his laughter.

"Hey, Neely," Jazzy spoke up, "wanna come with me to the cooler to get something to drink? I can't believe these idiots haven't been better hosts to you."

"Hey—I offered," Blake said, but it was lost on the both of us. I nodded so damn thankful to Jazzy I could've kissed her if she'd let me.

"Sure," I said, happily, "it's over here," I continued waving towards the other side of the stairs where I'd seen the guys getting their refills.

Once we were out of earshot, Jazzy spoke, "Listen, don't let the bitches run you off, Neely. It's what they want to do. Well, except for Amy, she totally stays to herself. Won't leave Jack's side all evening, I swear."

I shrugged, "Well, I figured as much, but I'm still trying to figure out why Seth invited me—hey, wait. Aren't those chicks your friends? I mean you all came together, right?"

She gave a derisive snort. "As if. No, just arrived at the same time. As for me, I'm here for Blake. He's a damn good guy."

"Yeah, I got that vibe. How long have you two been...together?"

She laughed softly. "We're not *together*—at least not in the way you think anyway. I'm his beard."

"You're what?" I asked, stopping in my tracks. "I don't understand what that means."

"Oh, you *are* a babe in the woods, aren't you?"

I visibly bristled. What the hell was this? Was I about to get another jab on being from Tennessee? I was about to snap at her, telling her to shut the hell up but she read me.

"Hold on, I'm not dissing on you at all. Actually, Neely, you are a breath of fresh air around here and I can tell that by hardly even knowing you. What I meant is that Blake is *gay*, all right? And in case you failed to notice, I'm *black*. A *beard* means a cover. Blake hasn't come out, and has no immediate plans to do so in the near future."

"Wait. Why not? What's wrong with him being gay? Especially here, I mean?"

"Yeah, well I get that it's 1997, Neely. But in some aspects, it might as well be 1957. Blake feels at this point in his career, it would be detrimental to come out. Look what happened when Ellen DeGeneres did it on her own damn television show? The network had a hissy fit."

I couldn't argue with that at all. "What about you?" I asked, "I mean about pointing out the fact that you're black?"

She sighed. "There is still a lot of bigotry in this country, even in laid back Southern California. What Blake offers me is a way in to a lot of the high-end parties...and barbecues," she pointed out, waving her arm towards the rest of the people at Seth's soiree. "And that helps me. I have goals too, and being part of the Malibu Brat Pack can only serve me well."

The Malibu Brat Pack?

Jazzy bent down and reached into the ice chest. "Wine cooler?" she asked, looking over her shoulder at me.

"Sure," I said, feeling at this moment I actually needed a bit of liquid courage. This was a lot of information for me to absorb. "But how can people like this particular crowd help you guys?" I asked, because let's face it, it was a question begging for an answer.

"Okay, fair question. So, listen up quickly. Seth is well connected, because obviously, both of his parents are in the industry. Julia over there? Yeah, her father is an A-List producer of feature films. Chloe's mother is an award-winning director, Jack's father is an agent, and Nelson's father is tied seven ways from Sunday to executives with two of the major filming studios in the country. And when you think about it, those connections have connections who have connections, and so on and so forth. Girl, it's all about who you know and who you blow in this industry."

My head was spinning with all the information she was tossing at me. "So what? You want to be an actress?" I asked, twisting the cap off of my wine cooler and taking a long swig.

"Not even close. No, I want to be a cinematographer. The best as a matter of fact. That's my dream, and my art. That's why Blake and I are best friends in all of this. I'm the beard, he's my connections. It works."

We started walking back and I was still trying to absorb all of this. I had no clue just how complicated and political the entertainment industry was, but I was sure my father was in the know. Damn, it had to be pretty cut throat I decided.

"So," Jazzy said, "we cool? This is like just between us, right?"

I nodded, "Oh yeah, no problem. Thanks for sharing and for being the only nice chick here tonight. Well, besides Amy," I clarified.

"Oh, and Neely?"

"Yeah?"

"You can always speak to me at school when we pass in the hallway."

"What?" I asked, stopping once again in my tracks, as my eyes widened, "You mean?"

"Uh yeah. I've seen you in the hall a few times. But hey, I don't take it personally. You always walk around with your head down. I don't know, it's like you wish you were anywhere but at Malibu High. I get it."

"Oh no," I said, feeling like a total piece of shit, "I'm just kind of in my own world, you know? I'm probably thinking about my drawing, painting, or my next custom montage. Painting is my lifeline. It's how I cope I think. So you're a senior too?"

"I am. And I will be so damn glad to graduate and then focus on my passion."

"Me too," I replied with a giggle, taking another swig. "Fuck Malibu High."

"I'll drink to that," she replied, tapping her bottle against mine. "Back to the party."

We had no sooner arrived back with the others than I could tell we'd been discussed during our absence.

A platter of burgers and brats was out on the table, and the others had evidently started eating. Seth was giving me the stink eye as if I'd shared last night with Jazzy to put a wrench in his relationship with Chloe. Fuck that.

"Better get the grub while it's hot," Blake called out, nodding towards the food. "Jazzy, you need to eat something, babe."

Okay. Definitely a beard.

"I'm on it baby," she called back, grabbing a plate. I was following behind her, and just as I picked up a plate, I could hear Julia and Chloe snickering from the lawn chairs that they'd taken next to one another.

I could tell by Julia's raised voice, this had been planned in advance. "So, Chloe," she said, "have you ever been to Tennessee? I hear it's beautiful."

I froze and waited. From beside me, I could tell that Jazzy was waiting for the punch line as well.

"No I haven't," Chloe replied, "but I hear they still iron their jeans down there," she finished, busting out in laughter. "That true, Neely?"

I felt Jazzy's hand as she placed it on mine. But no, this was the last fucking straw. I wasn't going to stick around and be the butt of their cruel fucking jokes.

I dropped my plate, and whirled around to face them all. Seth had a look of pure torture on his face, but he said nothing. Nelson was tossing Julia a dirty look. Julia was now looking down at her hands, not willing to face me. Jack had a look of shock on his face, and Amy was chewing on a fingernail. But Chloe? Chloe had a self-satisfied smirk on her face that turned my stomach.

Jazzy grabbed my arm as I started to move, but I shook it off. I gave one last look to Seth, and I'm not exactly sure what my expression told him, but it must've told him something because I saw it in his eyes. It was pure sadness and regret. But it wasn't enough to make me stay one second longer as I bolted towards my house.

I ran as if I had suddenly sprouted wings. Nothing but pure anger was the fuel. I heard nothing, I saw nothing. People could be so damn hateful. Some of them truly had black hearts, and I wanted none of it.

I was at the stairs leading up to my yard when I heard him.

"Neely! Neely! Wait, please Neely!"

I whirled around as Seth closed the distance between us, his breath now coming in pants. It was hard to believe that anyone with a sculpted and perfect physique such as Seth Drake would get winded keeping up with the likes of me.

"Please, Neely—"

"Shut up!" I shouted, my chest heaving with my exertion now. I could almost feel the adrenaline bubbling in my veins. "I hate you Seth Drake! And I regret every minute I ever wasted on liking you, let alone loving you! You are a despicable person! You claimed me last night, but now I'm un-claiming you as a person in my life! Don't you ever come near me again!"

And with that, I whirled back around and ran up the steps. Seth Drake would pay for the way he'd wronged me. That was a promise I made to myself.

Chapter 10

April 10, 1997

Spring Break

"How does it feel being an adult now, Neilah Grace?" my grandmother asked as she was driving me back to her place from the airport. It was spring break and there was no way I wanted to spend it in Malibu and risk running into Seth.

"It's not much different than when I was only seventeen, Grandma," I replied. "The good news is I got into Brantley College. I start in the fall. I can finally be out on my own."

"Where's this college located?" she asked.

"In Pasadena."

"Isn't that in California?"

"Well, yeah, Grandma, but I'm still going to live on campus. My friend, Jazzy, and I are getting an apartment together. She's going to study cinematography. I'm going to study art and photography."

"I see. Well, I'm glad you have a friend. Do you have a boyfriend?"

"No, Grandma. No boyfriend," I replied wistfully.

"What ever happened to that fellow you were sweet on a few years back? The one that lived down the road from your daddy; and sent those letters to you?"

My stomach lurched, the same way it always did when Seth's name passed someone's lips. And it happened more often than I would've liked. "That was over a long time ago, Grandma, remember? I broke up with him the last time I went out there to stay with Daddy for a few weeks that summer."

My grandmother gave a soft snort. "Nothing wrong with my memory, Neilah Grace. I knew that, but I thought maybe you eventually patched things up with him after the letters."

"Letters? What letters?"

She pulled her car into the parking lot of the house where my mother was now living. It was a group home of sorts, with a support staff there to assist people that had been treated for various addictions to help them maintain sobriety for as long as they felt they needed the assistance.

She turned off the ignition and looked over at me, her face lined with confusion. "After you returned home early that summer, you and your mama got your own place. A couple letters came to our house after you returned. I'm sure your granddaddy ran them out to your house."

I shook my head slowly. "Never got them," I replied.

"Oh well, water under the bridge now anyway, I expect. Now Neely, please be mindful on how you talk to your mama, you hear? She's well...she's better physically. Much stronger as a matter of fact, but she's still got some emotional healing to do."

I looked at my grandmother, wondering why in the hell she thought I'd do or say anything to upset Mama. "I want to see Mama get well. Why would I say anything to upset her?"

"It's just that she's not real happy with the fact that you're living out there with...*them.*"

"Grandma, what choice did I have? Surely Mama understands that, right?"

She nodded, but I could tell there was more. "She was very angry that I didn't put up a fight against your father to keep you here with me."

"Is that why she doesn't answer my letters? She's angry with me, too?"

"I think she's getting better, honey. I think once she sees you and knows that you're here for her—that you still love her best, she'll come to terms with the situation."

I released a hard sigh. "Great. Let's do this, Grandma."

Chapter 11

Grandma had been spot on with my mother's current condition. She did, in fact, look healthier and more alert than when I'd last seen her more than six months ago. She was also correct in that Mama still had an attitude about my living with Daddy and *that harlot*.

"So, Neely," Mama said sitting on a loveseat in the parlor of the group home, "has the harlot refurbished our home out there?"

"No, Mama," I lied, "It's pretty much the same. I redid a wall in my room since the corkboard is gone. It's my painting wall. I've got several creations up there already." I pulled a photo from my purse I'd taken with my camera to show her. "See here? What do you think?"

She took the photo from me and studied it for a few moments, her brow furrowed in confusion. "What in the world is that supposed to be?" she asked.

It was my 'Sin' montage. I'd finished it in record time after I'd called Seth out for his despicable behavior. I'd used symbols mostly, with some tattered faux-like drawings, which to anyone else's eyes would mean nothing, but to me, they were some of his features. Including his dick.

"It's called a montage, Mama. Just some symbolic stuff all mashed together with bits and pieces of things from memory."

"Well Neely, it certainly is...*busy*. Now, what's this thing here? Looks like some kind of a serpent?"

Oh geez...it was Seth's...

"Yes, Mama," I fibbed. "It's an evil serpent, very good."

"Well I never understood some of your paintings that you called...what was it, abstract?"

"It's okay, Mama. I understand them."

"So, how are things going for you out there, Neely? You like living there with your daddy and—"

I cut her off right then, I had to because I was tired of hearing the words whore, slut, floozy, harlot, and the host of other names she had for Tiffany. Oh, it wasn't as if I would ever bond with Tiffany—no way. But it was tiring to constantly hear my mother use that language.

"It's okay, Mama. I make do. Getting ready to leave for college in the fall. I'll be out on my own then."

Grandma shifted uncomfortably in her chair, giving me a silent shake of her head back and forth as if I shouldn't have divulged this bit of information.

Mama's eyes blazed pure anger. "What do you mean...college? You're not coming back home? You're *eighteen* now, Neely. Don't you think it's time for you to come on back here so we can be a family again? I mean it's not like I'll be living in Hamilton House forever! This is just a pit stop for me."

Clearly she was upset. But if she'd answered my letters or even read them, she might have had a clue as to what was going on in my life.

I looked over at my grandmother for help, but I could tell none was coming. "Mama, the plan has always been for me to pursue college, you know that. I have a partial scholarship to attend Brantley in Pasadena, and Daddy is paying the rest for me. It's an opportunity I can't afford to waste."

"Waste?" she all but shrieked, "Is that what I am to you Neilah Grace? Am I just a waste of your time and love?"

Grandma was getting distraught seeing Mama getting all upset over the topic, but I wasn't about pretending or being dishonest with my own damn mother.

"No, Mama, of course not. I just need to get my education so that I can have a career. That's always been the plan, nothing's changed."

She shook her head vehemently. "There are schools right here in Tennessee, Neely. Why in the world would you want to stay out in California? What's there that you don't have here?"

"Mama, it's too late to change anything now. It's done."

Mama was getting ready to spout something more, but blessedly, one of the counselors came to the door interrupting her. "Nina, it's time for group," the woman said, giving us all a friendly smile. "Your family is welcome to join us if they want."

"No," Mama snapped, "they were just leaving."

Grandma and I walked out to the car in silence. Just before she pressed the automatic lock, she looked over the roof of the car at me and spoke. "Neely, I'm sorry with how your mama responded in there. You do what you need to do for yourself. I raised Nina to be selfish I suppose, and I'm not gonna let her make you feel badly for living your life the way you see fit. You're turning out good, Child, that much I can tell. Will you forgive me for not being more supportive until now?"

I couldn't be angry or resentful of Grandma. I knew that she and my grandfather had done the very best they could raising Mama. "Grandma, I love you and I love Mama. But I think maybe Mama has some more healing to do, and that's not your responsibility or mine. She has to want to get better and to see life the way it really is for her now. Her anger and resentment are like a poison to her. I won't let her poison me any longer. I just can't do it."

We got into the car and she started it up. "When we get home, Neely, there're a lot of boxes I packed up when the landlord evicted your Mama. I want you to go through them over the next few days and separate anything you want me to keep from the apartment for you. I imagine your mama will be coming back to stay with me whenever she feels she can handle life again."

I nodded. "Okay, Grandma, I will. And thank you for understanding about my decision to stay in California. It's just something that I feel compelled to do."

Once back at Grandma's, I went down into her cellar and commenced going through the boxes that were piled in a corner with "Nina's Apartment" written in bold black marker on each side of them.

I never realized Mama and I had that much stuff. I thought most of my belongings had already been shipped out to California, and, for the most part, they had been. But the stuff in those boxes being stored in my grandmother's cellar were things I had no claim to personally.

I found one box full of photo albums that I hesitated before opening. Did I really want to revisit a past that no longer existed for any of us? I looked through the album that had been placed on the top, but soon discovered I wasn't ready just yet to go there, so I set it aside for the time being.

Most everything in there was, for the most part, memorabilia or things Mama would need if and when she ever set up residence on her own again.

The last box I opened was marked: Personal Items and Documents. This peaked my interest although I wasn't sure why. It contained mostly file folders that I never suspected Mama even kept. The manila folders were labeled with titles such as "School Records," "Bills," "Health Records," and then I came upon one that was labeled, "Personal Correspondence."

Who'd have ever thought Mama was that organized? I remembered all the past due bills, and shut-off notices we'd received because she hadn't been taking care of business towards the end of her descent into alcoholism.

Sure, while growing up, Mama was always organized and handled the bills until Daddy started making real money. Then he had an accountant who handled all of that plus the taxes, so Mama was no longer needed to be the administrator of those duties.

I wondered if that was one of the first triggers that set her off into drinking the way she had. Maybe she had started to feel unneeded in the roles she had previously assumed within the household. It was something to consider I suppose.

I opened the file labeled "Personal Correspondence" and leafed through stacks of papers, mostly those from her attorney during the divorce proceedings; some letters from Grandma to her, but then an envelope caught my eye, and then another one.

I recognized Seth's distinctive scrawl. Hell, I'd seen it so many times before, and, for a moment, I thought maybe it was the letters he'd sent to me, but I knew that I'd tossed them immediately upon returning to Tennessee after that summer visit with Daddy.

I looked at the front of the envelopes and, sure enough, they were addressed to me at my grandparents' home, but these were postmarked in July and August of 1994. After I'd left Daddy's early that summer.

I lifted the contents from the first envelope that had obviously already been opened. It was postmarked July 26, 1994. I unfolded the letter and began reading:

Neely,

I don't know what to say—or should I say write! I don't understand why you left. I found the letter you left me in my room, but it doesn't explain anything to me! Laura said that you were fine when you left, so I can't think it was anything she said or did to make you want to go back to TN. What is going on, Neely? Don't I deserve more of an explanation or something? I tried to call you, but your grandfather said you weren't there. He didn't say anything more. Did I do something to piss you off? Please tell me! I went to your father's house today because this is blowing my fucking mind. He acted like he's all pissed off and didn't tell me shit! This whole thing is so damn confusing. Please call me! We need to talk, Neely!

-Seth

I sucked in a hard breath. Oh my God, Seth had tried to contact me. All this time, I thought he hadn't really given a shit, or that his pride ruled. I felt numb.

I pulled the paper out of the second envelope. The one that was postmarked August 15, 1994.

Neely,

CLAIMED

I was...well, words couldn't describe what I was at the moment. Shocked? Confused? Angry?

I was all of those things and for different reasons.

My mother obviously had kept these letters from me for whatever reason. And I knew those reasons. She didn't want anything coming between my relationship with her as a daughter, but not because of her relationship with me. No, it was for the purpose of punishing my father for what she deemed as his betrayal of her.

Yeah, maybe he did betray her—no, there was no maybe. It was a fact: my father *had* betrayed my mother with his infidelity. But why the fuck had she made me pay the price for her anger towards him?

And then there was the matter of Seth. Yeah, I was somewhat appeased by the knowledge that he had tried to contact me; that he was bothered by my quick exit, and somehow that had triggered him to tell me in his letter that he loved me. But he'd never admitted that before. Why had it taken me walking out of his life to suddenly prompt that declaration?

How did I really know it was even a sincere feeling or simply a blow to his ego that he wanted to rectify? Besides that, he never did show up in Tennessee to find me and talk like he'd threatened to do in the second letter now had he?

It was all water under the bridge now, wasn't it? It was more than two years ago, but those years seemed like a lifetime when dealing with raw teenage emotions at such an impressionable age.

And given all of that, even if he assumed I'd read the letters and chosen to ignore them, it hadn't justified the cruel and insensitive treatment he'd dished out to me last winter.

His behavior towards me had been nothing more than revenge for something he decided I'd done—or in this case, not done—which had wounded his teenage pride and ego. What he'd done was unforgiveable.

What Mama had done should be unforgiveable, but I at least understood why she'd done it; and her state of mind back then wasn't what it should have been. Yeah, I could give Mama a free pass.

But not Seth.

Never Seth.

Chapter 12

June 3, 1997

Malibu High Graduation

Jazzy and I sat next to one another on the bleachers on the stage while the Dean of Students finished up his long, snoozer speech. I'd already had to jab Jazzy twice when she'd started to doze off.

"Thank God, he's finally wrapping this up," she whispered to me. "It's party time. You still coming to my house, right?"

I nodded. "As long as you know who isn't going to be there."

She rolled her eyes. "I already warned Blake. No worries."

"Shhh," a student in the row ahead of us said, turning around to glare at us.

Jazzy and I both made faces at her and she quickly rotated her head back around. We tried to stifle our giggles, but when the applause sounded signaling our final release from the Baccalaureate service, we just didn't give a damn about proper decorum.

We laughed like lunatics and quickly exited the bleachers and headed for the door.

"So, eight at my house?" Jazzy reminded me before she split to go over to where her family was waiting to take pictures.

"Yeah, I'll be there, but I'm warning you, if Seth and his bitch show up, you're never going to hear the end of it!"

She gave me a quick hug. "I told you, no worries!"

Dad and Tiffany walked up as Jazzy left, and my father was beaming with pride. "I'm so damn proud of you, Neely. But I can't help feel a bit sad knowing my girl is almost grown up."

"Almost?" I asked, quirking a brow. "Daddy, I'm there."

"No, not yet," Tiffany chimed in. "Not until you hit twenty-one officially."

Whatever, Tiffany.

"Party plans?" Dad asked, as we walked to his car. "Tiffany and I wanted to take you out to dinner."

"As long as we make it early. Have to be at Jazzy's house around eight. I'm the spending the night there too, okay?"

"That's fine. We'll make it an early dinner celebration then."

We were just finishing up what had turned out to be a fairly pleasant dinner, and awaiting dessert when Tiffany dropped the bomb.

"Did you hear the exciting news about Lotus Pointe?" she asked, a wide grin plastered on her overly made-up face.

"No, was it cancelled?" I asked, a faux concerned look on my face.

Her grin quickly faded. She knew I was being a bitch, but why should I care about her show? "No," she replied shortly, "Seth Drake signed a year's contract. He's replacing Julian next season. We start filming in July. I thought you'd be thrilled to see how he's launching his acting career in a prime time series."

I just bet you did.

"How wonderful for Seth," I said, the insincerity dripped from my words. "I suppose you have some credit coming for that move, right?"

Tiffany no doubt enjoyed playing the wicked stepmother role, and she did it so flawlessly.

"Well, I may have gotten him his foot in the door, but his audition spoke for itself. He's quite brilliant, and let's face it, those good looks of his didn't hurt either."

My father cleared his throat and quickly changed the subject to my upcoming move in the fall to Pasadena. He'd given me a nice check for graduation that would cover my portion of the rent for the upcoming school year, which for that, I was extremely grateful. Jazzy and I had found an apartment that would become available in August that we'd placed a security deposit on to hold it.

"So, are you going to work your part-time job over the summer?" Tiffany asked. "Seems like you might want to enjoy some time off before starting college."

I was a server at Antonio's Italian Cuisine off the Pacific Coast Highway, and, for whatever reason, the fact that I worked a job serving some of Tiffany's nearest and dearest friends somehow irritated her. It was as if she was embarrassed that I was slinging hash to earn some cash. Such a fucking elitist.

"Yeah, I'm gonna work until we move to Pasadena. Spending money is nice to have, Tiffany."

She rolled her eyes, and continued, "It's not like your daddy and I won't give you money, Neely. I mean *really*."

"Oh let her be, Tiff," Daddy warned. "It builds character. My first job in high school was washing dishes. What doesn't kill you makes you stronger, right Neely?"

"I guess," I mumbled, bored with the whole conversation. "Listen, Daddy, I'm gonna have to skip out on dessert. It's getting close to eight and I promised Jazzy I'd help her with the last minute stuff."

"Oh, okay," he replied, clearly disappointed. "Drive carefully. You aren't going to be drinking are you?" he asked.

"No, Daddy," I lied. "Her parents are going to be there to keep things PG-13, I promise."

"Good girl," he said with a smile and a wink. "Have a nice time."

I said my goodbyes and left, feeling a bit guilty for lying to him. Well, her parents were going to be home, that part was true, but as long as the kids were staying over and they handed over their car keys, the beer and wine would be flowing.

It wasn't as if I made a habit of drinking. In fact, I'd only done it maybe twice since I'd moved back last fall. I wasn't about to walk that same dangerous path my mother had, especially when alcohol dependency ran in families.

I'd have a beer or two and just enjoy socializing with friends and classmates I might never see again. It was a time of celebration and I'd earned the right to have one night in honor of this auspicious occasion, right?

Wrong.

Four hours later, I was drunk as a skunk in Jazzy's backyard. I'd staggered over into their humongous hedge maze on a dare that I could find my way into the center, where I had to grab a rosebud from the garden that was located there and bring it back out to prove I'd succeeded.

Only by the time I made it to the center, all I wanted was to pass out on the soft grass to sleep it off. I wasn't sure how long I was in there, but eventually, Blake sent someone in to rescue me.

CLAIMED

I was fairly sure it had been Seth; and I was pretty sure I fucked him right there in that stupid hedge maze.

81

Epilogue

April 17, 1998

Brantley College of Art & Photography
Pasadena, California

"Neely," Professor Andrews said, gazing at the collage I'd placed on the wooden easel for my presentation, "that's a very interesting choice of media you've selected. Not to mention risky."

"Risky?" I asked, quirking a brow in confusion. "How so?"

"Well, to start, you veered a bit from the assignment details which clearly articulated that everything was to be in black, white, or shades of grey. The lack of contrast was important. You've included some color in your abstracts."

"Only the eyes, Professor," I replied, standing back and admiring my work. "I couldn't bear not to show the ice blue of the eyes. It doesn't detract from the overall message though, does it?"

I watched as Professor Andrews cupped his chin, rubbing his fingers along the bristle of his neatly trimmed beard and considered my expressionist collage thoughtfully.

When he'd given this particular assignment, it had taken me all of a nanosecond to know which of my pieces I'd be using to compile the collage of emotional turmoil he'd outlined. And yes, I'd known that it was supposed to be void of color, but the eyes wouldn't have shown the emotion had I not brushed a pale shade of blue over them.

"I'll tell you what, Neely," he said, "stay after class and let's discuss this in a bit more depth, shall we?"

"Of course," I replied, taking my seat so that the next presenter could uncover his or her submission for this assignment. This was the third class in my year at Brantley School of Art & Photography I'd taken with Eric Andrews as my professor.

I knew him well. He was a superb teacher in every way. And yes, he was a stickler for adherence to detail on the projects he outlined and assigned for his classes, but he was also a fair and flexible man. Let's just say, we'd had issues like this before and always found common ground.

I'd stay after as requested. He'd pull a copy of the assignment details he'd provided to all of the students four weeks ago, and go over each one with me, point-by-point.

I'd sit at my table and remain silent as he ticked through each one, his deep, rich voice resonating the fact that he indeed had the upper hand in deciding whether or not my submission which had, technically, strayed from the parameters he'd set, would be accepted for credit.

In the end, he would allow me time to explain my reasoning for veering from the instructions, and defend my position as to why I felt it still complied with the overall spirit of the assignment, and therefore should be accepted for grading and credit.

He would ultimately concede, with a stern warning that I needed to focus more on adherence on future assignments. I would thank him for his consideration and flexibility, to which he would chuckle and tell me that it was now my turn to be flexible.

At that point, he would make sure the door to the art room was shut and locked. And then, he would pull me up from my seat against him. I would wrap my legs around his hips and allow him to carry me to a table or desktop, or maybe to a paint-splattered tarp that was heaped into a corner of the room. Whatever location he chose was where I would show him my flexibility.

Clothes would hurriedly be discarded in a frenzied fashion, and he would take me roughly, which I always demanded, and we'd fuck until we couldn't fuck anymore.

I knew the script by heart. We'd played to it more than once. Probably more like a dozen times over the past year. It still wasn't boring. Neither of us had grown tired of the foreplay we called Perspective Painting 201.

Everything unraveled just as usual. The classroom emptied, a couple of students lagged behind to suck up to him for projects presented this evening that were less than stellar. It was always pretty obvious. Eric did his best to assure them he would be fair and objective in his evaluation of their work.

Sure he would.

They were slackers.

They only took this class because they were required to as part of the curriculum for their Graphic Web Design certificate program. They had zero interest in art, expression, or theory.

At last.

We were alone.

Eric shut and locked the classroom door, and then quickly stalked over to where I was still sitting, gazing up at him. He was strikingly handsome with perfectly chiseled features and great body definition for a man whose career didn't involve physical labor of any sort. Dark brown hair and eyes. Fortyish with a scholarly look that his dark-framed glasses perpetuated nicely.

"So, Professor," I said in a throaty whisper. "Shall we debate the particulars of my non-compliance to the assignment once again?"

He didn't move any closer to me. In fact, he leaned back against the table in front of my desk, and stretched his legs out in front of him. His arms were crossed against his chest and he gazed at me for a moment, not saying a word.

This was different.

For a moment I worried if quite possibly he wasn't open to our usual negotiations. He surely wouldn't fail me on this assignment, would he?

"Why him?" he asked me, his eyes searching mine. "Why is it always him?"

"Wh-what?" I asked, my nose crinkled up in confusion. He was deviating from our normal script. What the hell was up with that? "I'm...I'm not following."

"For Christ's sake, Neely. No matter what the assignment, the required subject matter, the requested media, every goddamn one of your projects has some part of him included. Be it an eye, or lips, or a nose, or a full fucking face, it's always him. Why?"

"Why does it matter?" I flung back. "Art is subjective, right? Maybe he's my art. Maybe he's the only subject matter I've ever done right."

"So what? You simply keep drawing and painting him—or parts of him, over and over again in different themes, different styles, with different media rather than try something new? Something unique?"

I stood up quickly. "Every piece I've turned in to you has been freshly created! It's all been unique! It's not as if I keep turning the same pieces in over and over again, is it?" I was pissed now. What the hell was Eric trying to do? Why was he straying from the script?

"You might as well be turning the same piece in over and over again!" he shouted, startling me enough that I jumped. "I want you to turn something in, anything, that he's not a goddamn part of!"

I was shocked by his words, stunned by his anger. I backed away from where he sat, one arm outstretched behind me to make sure I didn't collide with a desk. "I don't understand. Why are you so angry with me, Eric?" I whispered.

He ran a hand through his mass of thick hair as if frustrated beyond his limit. "I'm not angry, Neely, I'm confused. Who the hell is this guy to you?"

I felt my muscles tense. My stomach clenched. I didn't have to share any of this with Eric Andrews. He had no right to even question me about it. It wasn't any of his business. His job was to teach and offer guidance and support for his students. His job was most certainly not to try to get into my head or to figure out what makes me tick, or why I chose the subject matter I did for my projects.

That was my shrink's job, right?

"Listen," I said, my voice holding a nervous lilt, "are you going to accept my submission for this assignment or not? I need to know."

He blinked a couple of times, still studying me as if his reading glasses had suddenly morphed into a powerful microscope that was unpeeling each and every layer of my psyche for his own personal examination.

"Yes," he finally said, releasing a heavy sigh. "It's accepted for grade."

"Okay then," I whispered, still watching him, a feeling of relief seeping over me. "So, are we going to fuck?"

He removed his glasses, and rubbed the bridge of his nose with his fingers, massaging away his obvious frustration. "No, Neely. No we're not."

I shrugged and grabbed my backpack from the top of my desk, and hoisted it up and over my shoulders. "Goodnight then, Eric. See you in class tomorrow," I replied as I left his classroom and headed out of the building.

It was just as well we stopped having sex anyway, I thought to myself as I walked along the paved parking lot toward my car. It had run its course, and in the scheme of things, it wasn't a long-term fit. I'd already concluded that a while back. Now I could focus fully on my curriculum.

My summer semester's course load was going to be a killer. It was all photography courses, but if I did well, there might be an internship available to me for hands-on experience. It was going to be killer for sure, but I relished the challenge. I longed for anything and everything to occupy a place in my mind. Thankfully, this would be my last class under Professor Andrews.

Literally.

Back at the apartment I shared with Jazzy, she was sprawled out on the sofa, munching popcorn with the television blaring. Her eyes flickered over me as I came through the door. "Early night with the professor?" she asked, giving me a naughty look.

Yeah, Jazzy knew about us, in fact, there wasn't much I didn't share with her. Best friends did that sort of thing, and she shared her deep dark secrets with me in return. At least I was pretty sure she did.

"Yeah, well I think our after class fuck fests are history, which is A-okay with me," I replied, plopping down beside her on the sofa and grabbing a hand of popcorn.

"Hey wait," she said laughing, "Where those hands been tonight, girlfriend?"

I laughed, and gave her a playful smack. "Shut up! I told you nothing happened. All he wanted to do was badger me about my choice of subject matter. Like always, he wanted me to explain my motivation. It's none of his damn business anyway."

She raised the remote and muted the television. "Well, it is kind of weird, Neely. I mean even I don't totally get it."

I popped some popcorn into my mouth and shrugged. "Well Jazzy, that makes two of us, I guess. I don't get it either, but it's just like that's all that comes to my mind when I draw or paint. Anything else just comes out looking like total shit."

"Have you told your shrink that?"

"Oh, right. That asshole? I gave him the boot too. All he wanted was to dwell on my estrangement from Mama. As if I can shed light on it since he obviously can't—I mean what the fuck? I'm not the one that shut her out of my life, now did I? She's the one that won't take my calls, doesn't answer my letters, and for all practical purposes has disowned me since I didn't go running back to Tennessee once I graduated. Grandma understands though. She tells me that every time we talk."

Jazzy reached over and brushed a lock of my now blonde hair from my face, "Hey, at least you have your grandma, and your dad, and even—oh shit!"

"What?" I yelled, jumping up and looking around to see if there was a spider in the vicinity. Jazzy had an irrational fear of all things multi-legged. There was nothing I could see crawling on the sofa or floor.

"No," she said, laughing, "I just remembered your stepmother called here. She needs to talk to you urgently. You need to call her ASAP. Oh, I had to listen to her go on and on about you not having a cell phone and how you need to come into the 90's, blah, blah, blah."

I went over to the kitchen wall phone, calling back to Jazzy. "She didn't say if it was an emergency with my dad or anything, did she?"

"She didn't give me any details except it was urgent she talk to you as soon as possible. I'm sure you're dad is okay, Neely."

I dialed her cell number and waited for her to pick up, leaning against the kitchen wall and twisting the long, stretched beyond its means phone cord.

"Neely?" she asked immediately. She had Caller I.D.; she knew who the hell was calling.

"Yeah, what's up?"

"We have a situation at the studio, and I could really, *really* use your help."

My brow furrowed. What kind of a situation at her studio could possibly require my help? "What is it?"

And within two minutes, I was sorry I asked, and I was even more sorry I'd returned her fucking phone call. Somehow,

I allowed my wicked stepmother to whine, beg, guilt, and even cajole me into doing her a big, big favor.

Apparently, whomever the chick was that played opposite Seth's character—Austin whatever the last name was, had been in a car accident and was in the hospital getting ready to undergo surgery on several broken bones. There was one key scene left to film for the season finale of Lotus Pointe.

Since I was the same height, build, and my hair color and length matched that of the actress who was laid up, Tiffany had promised the producers I would fit the bill in doing that scene, with Seth, as long as it was shot from behind.

What the ever-loving hell?

"It's only one line and they can cut her voice in and replace yours in post-production," she said. "Neely, it will take about two hours of your time, and I went out on a limb here. I promised you'd do it."

That had totally pissed me off. "You had no right to do that, Tiffany," I hissed over the phone.

It was when it sounded as if she were crying that my last line of defense crumbled. I capitulated. She was ever so grateful and gave me the time and building I was to report to the following day. She assured me the guard at the gate would have my pass and badge to allow me access to the set.

Much later, after I had shared all of this with Jazzy, and she had done her best to convince me that everything would be okay, I allowed my mind to drift.

I hadn't seen Seth since the night of my drunken stupor at Jazzy's party. At the time, I hadn't been sure if it had been Seth there with me, but Jazzy assured me the following day that it had, in fact, been him. I hadn't touched a drop of alcohol since then.

"Oh my God," I had moaned, the morning after the party as Jazzy had held my hair up while I puked for the third or fourth time. I'd lost count. "I'm pretty sure we had sex there in that rose garden."

"Duh" she exclaimed, and then laughed so hard she was practically rolling.

"Please, Jazz, I don't want to know," I replied, flushing the toilet and standing up on wobbly legs to rinse my face and mouth.

"Girlfriend, we could hear y'all going at it behind those shrubs, I swear!"

"Uh uh," I argued, shaking my head. "No you didn't."

"Uh, *yeah* we did. You two were gettin' *down* from the sounds of it. Blake said you both were moaners," she finished, starting to giggle uncontrollably once again.

"Oh, shit," I groaned. "What the hell had *he* been thinking? Shoot, what the hell had *I* been thinking?"

She shook her head, still grinning like a fool. "He wanted pussy. You wanted dick. S'all good. I think that last shot of Wild Turkey did you in."

And now, as I fought to find sleep, I wondered if maybe Seth had been just as wasted as I was that night.

If I were lucky, maybe he didn't recall the entire incident at all. At least that's what I hoped. It wasn't possible for me to ever forget that night. The repercussions from it had hit me full force before I even left for Pasadena last August.

I rolled over in bed, and buried my head under my pillow to drive it all from my mind. It was too painful, still too fresh even though it had been nearly a year since the last night I'd seen Seth Drake.

And as always, whenever the bits and pieces of that night—our last time together—crept into my mind, a dull ache gnawed in the pit of my stomach, and I was overwhelmed by the emptiness and despair I was left with once the pain subsided.

End of Book 2! But keep reading!

Sneak peak of book #3 - Then keep going!

SYNOPSIS:

"Are you ready for your close-up, Mr. Drake?"

Book 3 in the Evermore Series finds Neely Evans enjoying a lucrative career, but not the one she aspired to as a child. Neely is one of the top, most sought after celebrity photographers, freelancing her expertise to the highest bidding tabloids. In the world of *paparazzi,* Neely is known as the clever and elusive "Grace Evangelista."

Seth Drake has hitched his rising star to Julia Cantrell, a Hollywood actress with the best connections in the business. But Seth's life has a void Julia will never fill. He can't shake Neely from his mind, and though he doesn't know it, the same applies to her. Neely has a bond with Seth that no amount of time or distraction will ever erase. But it's . . . complicated. Then again, it's never been simple where Neely Evans and Seth Drake are concerned.

Adult Content 17+

Paparazzi Excerpt

I was crouching behind a shrub line next to the tennis courts of a huge estate on Mulholland Drive. Fourth of July weekend in lovely Malibu, California. My old stomping grounds. This was my first solo shoot, and I was determined I wasn't going to fuck it up by not getting the pic, or worse yet, getting busted for criminal trespassing. Jerry was testing me and I sure as hell wasn't going to blow it my first time out.

There was a big party going on. Loud music. Lots of people. Lots of drinking. Lots of coke being snorted. The more wasted they all got, the easier it would be for me to get close enough to blend in and not outed for the party crasher I was.

I unzipped the flap on my fanny pack and removed my 'EOS Kiss III' camera. This baby had only come out in April, but it was meant for what I do. Auto-focusing, thirty-five zone metering, and night lens photography. Plus it was compact. It only weighed three quarters of a pound with batteries.

I'd had a close call while climbing over the fence on the other side of the tennis court, after I'd disabled the security camera nearby. I'd learned a trick for that from Jerry. There's actually a way to disable those bad boys without it sending a signal to the security panel inside. It involves a squirt gun, some vinegar, a tiny bit of baking powder and—no, never mind. I really shouldn't be discussing tricks of the trade. I remembered Jerry had cautioned me against that from the start of my internship with him.

Should I back up? Did you miss it? I had a new career as of May 1st of this year. That's right.

I was now a celebrity photographer.

I am...paparazzi.

Yeah, Malcolm had pitched a bit of a fit, but I promised him I could freelance for his agency whenever my schedule permitted. He'd finally come around, wishing me the best and ensuring me that I was with the best for the career I was entering. I promised him it wouldn't be forever, because that was a promise I'd already made to myself.

I couldn't complain at all. The money, even during my internship, was pretty damn good. The solo money would be twice as much. Jerry loved it that I could process my own film as well. No worries that some PhotoMat® developer would scarf up the photo and make tracks to a tabloid before we got our pictures back, or worse yet, make duplicates and go to several tabloids.

"Don't think that hasn't happened before," Jerry had told me, thoroughly agitated. "Some people have no moral compass," he finished, shaking his head in disgust.

Jazzy and I had moved into a rental condo just off of Santa Monica Blvd. Yep, it was a real step or two up and we loved it, though it didn't come cheap.

Just then I heard some footsteps heading in my direction from the lawn. I peeked through the shrubs.

Damn!

Luck must be my middle name. It was my mark, and she wasn't alone. Everyone knew Devon Donnelly, the star of Primrose Place. Another nighttime soap that had hit the big time over the last few years. She was a femme fatale that loved the spotlight, and what she loved more than that was her wealthy husband's money and all that it afforded her.

Parties like this, for example, whenever he was directing a film in Europe. Yeah, she was married to none other than Truman Romanski, the most sought after director in the business. He was forty years her senior, but what he lacked in looks and apparently...dick, he made up for with his hefty bank account.

We'd caught wind that while Romanski was filming in Europe, Devon was playing hard and loose.

Another photographer had caught her leaving the Hard Rock last night on the arm of her latest co-star, Ricky Havana, and had snapped some candid shots of the couple.

Problem was, Havana had broken the paparazzi's camera, and then his jaw. Whomever Devon was entertaining tonight wasn't Havana. He'd been locked up for criminal assault, and, as of two hours ago, even though his bond had been posted, the dude was refusing to leave the jail. Said he was going to make a political statement about invasion of privacy or some such shit.

Didn't celebs realize that with their fame and fortune came public interest—and even scrutiny? Whoever told them that fame was free?

End of Sneak Peek!

About Andrea Smith

Andrea Smith is a USA Today Best-Selling Author of more than thirty works of fiction. She has a wicked sense of humor, and no matter the genre, she is able to infuse laughter throughout.

Here is a listing of her published fiction to date:

CLAIMED

DREAM SERIES
(New Adult Romance/Suspense/HEA)
These Books should be read in order:

SHADOWS AND DREAMS (Book 1)

"That was definitely hot," I said, propping myself up on an elbow to look at him, "going all 'Christian Grey' on me like that."

"Who?" he asked, totally clueless...

I wasn't prepared for what was in store for me when I took a summer position at Sinclair Stables before my junior year of college. After all, it could only help with my chosen field of equine studies, right?

My first encounter with Trey Sinclair wasn't a pleasant one to say the least. I didn't realize he was taking time away from his law firm in Atlanta to oversee his family's business in Bristol Virginia over the summer. He was definitely an alpha who liked exerting his power . . . and his prowess.

And then there was all this weirdness going on there. Like something from a Hitchcock movie! I was there with baggage I didn't realize I had! Trey Sinclair turned out to be my protector . . . and so much more!

Adult Content. 18+

THESE DREAMS (Book 2)
Think "pink" Mr. Sinclair! There's a new girl in your orbit!

'These Dreams' is the second installment in the *'Dream Series'* and finds Trey Sinclair and Tylar Preston, his fiancée, new parents to an adorable baby girl!

But as their wedding day approaches, Tylar is once again haunted by recurring nightmares that leave her fearful for the safety of her baby. She struggles to unravel her past with the help of a psychologist at Trey's insistence. Together they delve back into Tylar's childhood which opens the door allowing her to secure her future happiness. All is not without cost and there are plenty of surprises along the way.

Their journey together is often rocky with unexpected twists and turns along the way; their passion is relentless. They give each other strength during the difficulties they encounter with friends and family in this continuing story of their love and commitment.

ADULT CONTENT.

SHATTERED DREAMS (Book 3)
Life's About Love . . . And Life's About Pain . . .

My life was about to get even better! Trey and I had a new home, complete with horses for me to train. Preston was growing leaps and bounds; and so happy to have a baby brother or sister on the way. Tristan and Gina had just welcomed their new son into the family.

All was good.

But sometimes life can deal a bad hand or two and you don't see it coming. A sudden loss. A fractured marriage. A separation to clear one's mind or reset priorities. To examine one's heart and soul.

I will always love Trey. Trey will always love me.

But is that enough?

Book 3 in the "DREAM SERIES" is the Author's favorite of the bunch. Read it. You will see why.

CLAIMED

DREAM LOVER (Book 4)

Being Tylar's best friend wasn't nearly as easy as I made it look. Keeping my secret past from Tristan was even harder.

Book 4 in the 'Dream Series' is Gina's story.

And it's a surprising one. Maybe Gina isn't the tough cookie she appears to be . . .

My name is Gina Valenti Hatton, and I'm an East Coast girl. I'm Italian, a bit outspoken, and to those who know me, I'm tough as nails.

I live a lie.

There's a part of me that is terrified that he'll find me. And now that I'm with Tristan Sinclair, all thoughts of my past are starting to fade. But Tristan knows I'm keeping something from him, and when my darkest fear shows up, my only hope is that we can survive my past.

.

It is important to read the three prior books in the 'Dream Series" prior to reading Book 4.

105

ALPHAS IN LOVE SERIES
(Contemporary Romance/Suspense/HEA)
Can be read as standalones, but are most enjoyable if read in order.
SLATE (Book 1)
Fate hasn't always served Samantha Dennison well.

A shotgun wedding when she was just 16 years-old to a man who has been cold and distant at best, Samantha devoted herself to raising their only child, Lindsey for as long as she could.

But now, Lindsey is away at college and Samantha can no longer deny her empty life, and doormat existence. At 35, she is desperate to carve out an identity for herself and shoot some adrenaline into her tattered self-esteem. It is with that purpose in mind, she signs up for pole-dancing lessons, never imagining this single decision will change her life forever.

People close to Samantha would never have guessed the soccer mom they once knew could transform herself so flawlessly into the seductive "Diamond," a pole dancer at a Gentleman's Club in Indianapolis. "Diamond" becomes the object of one biker's attention, and as much as she tries not to cross that line, fate once again intervenes, and this time she's fully prepared.

If you enjoy romance, twisty suspense, and second chances at true love, this book will not disappoint!.
ADULT CONTENT

TRACE (Book 2)

Our futures are left to fate. And if we're lucky, sometimes fate throws us a curve ball we couldn't possibly have seen coming.

USA Today Best Selling Author Andrea Smith brings an unlikely pairing in Book 2 of the "G-Man Series."

Nineteen year old Lindsey Dennison returns home after her freshman year of college to find the life she had left existed no more. Her parents' marriage had imploded; her dad was on the run from the law, and her mother had somehow found her lost youth.

All in less than a year's time.

Enter twenty-nine year old Taz Matthews, a sexy FBI agent and partner of her new stepfather, and suddenly Lindsey's life is about to get really complicated.

When Lindsey's safety and well-being are threatened, Agent Taz is sent to protect her. The problem is, there's nobody to protect Taz when he finds himself becoming smitten with the sweet and innocent Lindsey.

Trying to fight the urge proves useless for this hot FBI agent and stuff is about to get real! He finds himself in uncharted territory with Lindsey Dennison. All he knows is that somebody is out to take what he now claims as his . . .

EASTON (Book 3)

Running away from a broken heart, something new to her, the beautiful, privileged and spoiled Darcy finds herself on a far away beach when she sees him.

This beautiful man watching her from down the beach, while he's with another woman. His eyes are only on Darcy. The beginning of something harsh, but extraordinary is about to start . . . and neither one of them will have the power to stop what draws them together.

He is gorgeous.

He is sexy.

He is broken.

He is strong.

He catches her eye in a mirror . . .

Her eyes meet his . . .

She reminds him of someone from his past. And she wants him very much

And it all ***BEGINS***.

CLAIMED

ALPHA CRUISE (Book 4)
On the first day of vacay . . .

Spend the holidays with the G-Men, their women and extended family as they cruise the Caribbean in first class accommodations compliments of Easton Matthews!

This book will give the reader an entertaining read, with the usual unpredictable circumstances, along with misunderstandings, love and lots of humor! You will read chapters from each character's point of view, and learn a few things about some of the characters you didn't know.

Along with that, there are bonus chapters, along with a secret "gag" chapter meant only to shock my editor, I promise.

ANDREA SMITH

TAZ (Book 5)
"Is he alive?"

USA Today Best Selling Author Andrea Smith brings you your favorite G-Man in this next installment in the G-Man Series!

Trace "Taz" Matthews has it all: a thriving career with the FBI, a gorgeous wife, Lindsey, and two beautiful children. Life doesn't get any better than this for him.

UNTIL one day, when he's asked to temporarily leave his position within the BAU, to handle an undercover mission that is blanketed in secrecy, even within the Bureau. It's a decision he may live to regret when unexpected circumstances cause him to be injured. His injury has far-reaching effects, not only with his life, but with the Bureau, and in particular—his marriage.

You will have all of the suspense, intrigue and steaminess that you've come to expect from . . . Taz.

WESTON (Book 6)
Holy Hockey Puck!

Weston Matthews is 21, a senior in a prestigious, Ivy League College, and has a tongue like Gene Simmons! He's a frat boy, hockey jock, and all around ladies man. He does have one problem though, he has to ace his Early American Lit class in order to graduate and stay eligible to play hockey for Hardwick University.

Weston is provided a tutor to help with his senior Lit class. Enter Penny Lane, also a senior at another local college, doing part-time status at Hardwick. She tutors to earn money, but her aspirations go far beyond just that. Penny is plain, nerdy, brilliant, and has a hidden agenda. She and Weston get off on the wrong foot, and from there, things will only get crazier.

Fasten your seat belts, and hold on for dear life as you take this roller-coaster ride on the Walk of Shame!

BRYCE (Book 7)

Bryce Slater is eighteen. He's a bad boy hottie who has his pick of chicks. He parties a bit. Smokes a little dope now and then. Likes the occasional random hook-up. So what? He's determined NOT to follow in his father's FBI footsteps.

Avery Sinclair is 19. She's in college, and during the summer she works on her grandparents' horse stables and race track as team leader. She takes her work seriously. Her future is in equine operations. She has no time for slackers on her team. But thanks to her uncle doing a favor for a friend, Avery ends up with Bryce Slater for the summer.

"Slater the Slacker" soon becomes Avery's pet name for him, but damn if she isn't determined to whip him into shape. And while doing so, she finds herself inexplicably drawn to him. *But he's so not her type!*

Bryce Slater quickly gets on the bad side of his new boss, saucy little half-pint Avery Sinclair. She's a sexy little spitfire who is determined to break his spirit. But in the process, Bryce finds himself inexplicably drawn to her. *But she's so not his type.*

What started out to be a summer of tough love punishment, turns into something both Bryce and Avery never expected. Just as things are heating up, a blast from Bryce's past threatens the fragility of his new found relationship with Avery.

CLAIMED

CARSON: THE UNTOLD STORY (BOOK 8)

Sometimes life is just too damned complicated.

I long to stand at the precipice of my existence, watch my whole life replay in front of me in bold, neon, polychromatic flashes from a kaleidoscope that shows my story so I can see how it all finally ends. My aspirations are high, but almost always met. It's the thing I do.

It's who I am, or maybe it is who I *used* to be.

Carson Renee Matthews.

Second child and only daughter of Easton & Darcy Matthews

I've been through an horrific experience, one that left me clinging to life in the hospital. Everyone has questions. I don't have the answers to give them. You see, I have no clue as to the details leading up to my *accident*. But there are people out there that have the answers, and I'm determined to find them - *before they find me.*

Enter Krew Beckett. My former physical therapist who becomes much more than that after he unexpectedly shows up in my life again once I return to campus at Columbia University. But is Krew hiding secrets, or am I simply afraid to trust anyone?

Come take this journey with me.

TRIPLE PLAY (Book 1)
M/M/F ROMANCE W/HEA (Men Series)

Paige Matthews has a lot to learn - about everything, including herself. At age twenty-two, Paige finds herself driving across the country to start an internship with the F.B.I. in Quantico, Virginia.

Having been "pushed from the nest," she is not at all enthused about being under the watchful eye of her older brother, FBI Agent Taz Matthews. She does her best to put things in turmoil, and it isn't long before she finds herself looking for new roommates.

Enter lovers Eli Chambers and Cain Maddox who recently purchased a house and are looking for somebody to help with the bills. It seems as if everything is fitting into place finally for Paige.

Until something happens between her and the guys. The ones she lives with; the ones she loves.

This is no typical "Three's Company" story though. Paige embarks on a journey of self-discovery that teaches her not only about giving, but accepting love as well. She soon realizes that sometimes what you're searching for has been right there with you all along.

CLAIMED

DOUBLE HEADER (Book 2)

Will Eli do the right thing, or put their three-way relationship at risk?

This sequel to "Triple Play," finds Paige, Eli and Cain trying to add to their family. Unfortunately, they've been trying for several months with no luck. The stork seems to be ignoring them . . . or is he?

When an unexpected person shows up on their doorstep, it isn't quite the bundle of joy they've been hoping for, but their lives are about to get even more interesting. Someone from Eli's past is about to play havoc with their summer, and put a crimp in their love lives.

Steamy, sexy, and an incredibly complicated scenario is about to play out, that finds Eli caught between a rock and a hard place (pardon the pun).

LIMBO SERIES
(Contemporary Steamy Romance with Paranormal Edge/HEA)
SILENT WHISPER
What does a mob capo want with a girl from the sticks?
Everything . . .

For twenty-seven years, I've flitted through life clueless to the God-given abilities that lay dormant inside of me. In the blink of an eye, everything changed more than I ever could've anticipated.

She changed it.

Now I know that nothing is as it seems. I will never be the same again...but this isn't my story.

It's hers.

I'm just being forced to live it, resolve it, and ultimately try to move on after learning that our lives are going to be tangled far more than I would've ever imagined.

My name is Parrish Locke. And I can see the dead.

CLAIMED

STOLEN DREAMS (BOOK 2)
I had some dreams they were clouds in my coffee . . .

It's 1974 in Evanston, Wyoming. Cece Adams, a popular cheerleader loves her bad boy next door, Erik Laughlin, a local rocker. They've had their share of ups and downs, but things have turned around for them. They have their dreams after all. And Cece has some news for Erik.

But Erik never gets the news because Cece never arrives at his Valentine's Day gig. There's been a car accident and Cece is dead.

Fast forward forty years . . .

Parrish Locke, a 27 year-old model has only recently discovered she has a gift. It's a spiritual one she sometimes wish she didn't have. It's . . . complicated. But when stalled souls reach out to her, she can't say no to helping them resolve their unfinished business.

Stolen Dreams finds Parrish back in the 1970's, in the small Wyoming town where Cece lived and died as a result of a car accident one snowy night. But Parrish knows this isn't what really happened. After forty years, how will she convince authorities there is more to the story?

One relationship fizzles, while a new one sizzles!

FORBIDDEN SERIES
(New Adult- Taboo/HEA)
Need to be read in order.
CROSSING LINES (Book 1)
When is love wrong?

Jesse Ryan has always been the love of my life, from as far back as I can remember. But time, distance and circumstances beyond my control separated the two of us for many years.

Now things have changed. Because you see now I'm a grown woman, and it's time that Jesse sees that for himself. But will he see me as anything other than the child I was when we last saw one another? It's up to me to make sure that he does.

Look out Jesse Ryan. September is back.

ANDREA SMITH

THE LOVE EFFECT (Book 2)

My name is Jesse Ryan. I'm thirty, single, and raising my daughter alone. I'm a construction worker in Arkansas, and in the summer of 2010, I knew I'd need some help with my nine year-old daughter, Scout. That's when September Dawson came back into my world.

She's a beautiful woman now, and a very resourceful one at that. She effectively ambushes a romance that is barely off the ground between me and a neighbor and she doesn't stop there. Suffice it to say by summer's end, I'm hers in every way. Yeah, I get that there's an eleven year age difference, but despite my better judgment and solid resolve, *the heart wants what the heart wants.*

And that brings us to now.

We've managed to keep our relationship discreet, but at the same time, planning our future together. *Then we get . . . the news.* And everything we've been planning is suddenly and inexplicably torn from us. After more six years without a word, my estranged wife, Libby, resurfaces. She has been seriously injured and now suffers from total amnesia. She doesn't remember any of us.

Now decisions need to be made, and everyone looks to me to be the one to make them. But how can I make a decision that will be in everyone's best interest?

SOUTHERN COMFORT
(NA SUSPENSE)

Welcome to Layton, Alabama. Population 11,000. Where the sweet tea runs through our veins, the air smells of cobbler, and the secrets lie so deep that not even the confessionals are safe anymore.

My name is Sunny Gardner. And Layton is my home, or least it had been until Avery Dawson came into our lives. They say that evil comes in all forms, but nobody in Layton expected evil would come to us as a minister who preached the Word, but lived a lie.

CLAIMED

This is my story. A story of struggle and triumph and, ultimately, how I saved myself and my community from the devil himself.

Adult Content 17+

EVERMORE SERIES
(NA Romance/Suspense)
This is a 4-set serial of novellas following boy next door first love, through the years to a second chance romance. Must be read in order.
CRUSHED (Book 1)
We were just kids when we met. . .
He was the boy from down the beach.
I was the transplant from Tennessee.
He became my best friend.
I became his best girl.
And then . . . it became us.
We shared things . . . our dreams, our secrets . . . first kisses and then our hearts.

Seth Drake was my everything. My first crush. My first love. My forever passion. Until that day when everything changed through no fault of ours.

I was crushed. We were crushed.

CLAIMED

CLAIMED (Book 2)
Love should be everything or not at all.
At least that's what I used to think.

I'm seventeen now, and back in Malibu. Mama's drying out back East, and here I am living with my father and his new wife, Tiffany Blume, Hollywood harlot. At least that's what Mama calls her. I keep my distance. I just have to bide my time until I turn eighteen and go off to college. Away from them; away from Seth Drake.

Seth is living his dream. Studying acting in New York City, landing a recurring role in a hit series, and grabbing my heart one last time until it breaks.

He's got fame. Fortune will likely follow.

I hate him.

I love him.

ANDREA SMITH

PAPARRAZI (Book 3)
Chase you till you're mine . . .
"Get ready for your close-up Mr. Drake."
I've found a career. Or maybe a career has found me. It's one I never would have imagined; one that I've never respected. But yes, I am paparazzi now in one of the most flush communities in the country. My reputation is well-known. When the tabloids need the shot, I'm the one that delivers.
I am Grace Evangelista.
I'm really Neely, but a cover is essential in my business. And Seth Drake is about to get up close and personal with my expertise. Is it revenge I want? Or is it simply validation that yes, I can be as good at my craft as he is at his? Whatever the reason, he's about to be blown away. Sometimes the best laid plans go awry for something better.
This just might be one of those times . . .

CLAIMED

STAR F*CKING (Book 4)

"Neely, I'm putting my foot down, babe. You are coming with me while I do this film, because there's no fking way I'll be apart from you again."**

Book 4 is the conclusion of the Evermore Series.

Seth and Neely's paths have crossed over the years, but not in the way they had hoped. The misunderstandings between them stem from issues beyond their control, but the truth will be revealed.

No matter who the players are that come in and out of their lives, one thing cannot be denied: Seth and Neely are meant to be together. Their love is destined to endure.

Almost anything.

ANDREA SMITH

DREAM SERIES BOX SET

Trey Sinclair always gets his way. That is, until he meets Tylar...

Atlanta attorney Trey Sinclair always gets what he wants whether it's in the courtroom, the bedroom, or on his family's horse farm. But when a bombshell is quite literally dropped into his lap, he can't help but be drawn to the feisty, independent, and strictly off limits Tylar Preston.

But Trey never takes no for an answer and Tylar desperately tries not to break her own rules.

It's only a matter of time.

They both know it.

What they don't expect is their intense and irresistible passion or the danger Tylar finds herself in because of a secret from her past.

Dream Series Box Set is a complete series bundle. Four full-length novels filled with excitement, mystery, and steamy surprises from *USA Today Bestselling Author Andrea Smith.*

Here's what readers are saying:

"I really really loved this series, Andrea just blows me away at anything she writes. But this series is a must read, promise you will not be disappointed!"- ***Sammie's Book Blog***

MATURE CONTENT: This story contains sexually explicit material, mature subject matter, and is intended for individuals over the age of eighteen.

CLAIMED

Don't miss out!

Visit the website below and you can sign up to receive emails whenever Andrea Smith publishes a new book. There's no charge and no obligation.

https://books2read.com/r/B-A-DYO-CCSLB

BOOKS 2 READ

Connecting independent readers to independent writers.

Did you love *Claimed*? Then you should read *Paparazzi*[1] by Andrea Smith!

[2]

"Get ready for your close-up Mr. Drake." I've found a career. Or maybe a career has found me. It's one I never would have imagined; one that I've never respected. But yes, I am paparazzi now in one of the most flush communities in the country. My reputation is well-known. When the tabloids need the shot, I'm the one that delivers. ***I am Grace Evangelista, the most notorius paparazzi in the Greater L.A. area!*** (I'm really Neely, but a cover is essential in my business.) And Seth Drake is about to get up close and personal with my expertise. Is it

---

1. https://books2read.com/u/47lpVg

2. https://books2read.com/u/47lpVg

revenge I want? Or is it simply validation that yes, I can be as good at my craft as he is at his? Whatever the reason, he's about to be blown away.

Sometimes the best laid plans go awry for something better.This just might be one of those times . . .ADULT CONTENT

Read more at www.andreasmithauthor.com.

Also by Andrea Smith

ALPHAS IN LOVE
Slate
Trace
Easton
Cruisin' With the G-Men
Taz
Weston
Bryce

Beyond Series
Broken Dreams

Dream Series
Shadows & Dreams
These Dreams
Shattered Dreams
Dream Lover

Evermore Series
Crushed
Claimed
Paparazzi
Star F*cking

G-Man
Carson: The Untold Story

Limbo
Silent Whisper
Stolen Dreams

M/M ALPHAS
Blacklisted
Quid Pro Quo

MMF Sandwich
Triple Play
Double Header

Naughty Nuggets
Santa's Stocking Stuffers

Standalone
Men Duet
Southern Comfort
Dream Series Box Set
Bitch Games: We All Play Them
The Other Man
Wasted
Hard Balled
All of Me
Maybe Baby Box Set
Love in Limbo

Watch for more at www.andreasmithauthor.com.

About the Author

Andrea Smith is a USA Today Best-Selling Author of New Adult Romance, Romantic Suspense, and Contemporary Romance with an erotic tone. She also writes naughty nuggets with Laurel Landon!

Check out her other books! You will never be bored!

Read more at www.andreasmithauthor.com.

www.ingramcontent.com/pod-product-compliance
Lightning Source LLC
Chambersburg PA
CBHW020722160726
47993CB00006B/2309